Unshakable Dreams

Unshakable
DREAMS

a novel

Dreams Trilogy – Book 3

Elizabeth Ann Thompson

Visit elizabethannthompson.net & pursueyourdreams.net to contact the author.

Publishing Consultant: AuthorPreneur Publishing Inc.—authorpreneurbooks.com

Editor: Alissia J.R. Lingaur
Cover Designer: Zizi Iryaspraha Subiyarta
Interior Designer: Amit Dey—amitdey2528@gmail.com

ISBN: 979-8-9916199-4-3 (paperback)
ISBN: 979-8-9916199-5-0 (ebook)
ISBN: 979-8-9916199-6-7 (audiobook)

To my grandmothers, Ethel and Ruth,
who shared home and heart and gifts of
writing and creativity. You both hold a
special place in my heart.

Also by Elizabeth Ann Thompson

Unforgotten Dreams
Secret Dreams

Nash yanked the black phone off the wall. His voice boomed, "Yeah?" Echoes ricocheted within the barn. He let the metal bucket filled with oats he'd been carrying drop. Dust and chaff floated in the sunlit air. His gray eyes traveled to the cement floor as he ran a hand over his dark brown crew cut.

A familiar voice on the other end of the line sparked his irritation. "Nash. It's me. I only have one call."

"Don't even start." Nash shouted and flicked off the prickly hay stuck to the collar on his Carhartt jacket. "Do you even know what you've put me through? You left a mess." He glanced out the open barn door and watched two robins bobbing for worms in the yard on a chilly spring day in April. "I hope you're happy in your cushy jail cell out in Wyoming." He grunted. "Where I'm supposed to be. My boss is on my case about moving the cattle to higher grazing." He looked upward as his head bent back. "I'm happy to help but what you've done has put me in a bind."

Hank's voice cracked through the receiver. "Nash. I only have one call. Just listen."

One of the horses thumped his hoof against a stall wall and snorted.

"I'm not in the mood for listening right now. If you had told Miranda about your legal situation and had taken care of things in the first place, we wouldn't be in this tornado."

"What tornado?"

Nash's lips tightened in a straight line.

"Nash. Buddy. What's going on? What happened?"

"Don't buddy me." He grumbled. "Your wife had her baby, you idiot."

"What?"

A guy in the background muttered. "Hurry up, I gotta call my dad to get me out of here."

Hank grumbled. "Just a minute, man."

Nash heard desperation and tears in Hank's voice, and he softened. "Your wife had a baby girl."

"Little Emily." He sniffled. "How are they? It was a month early. Are they ok?"

Another guy yelled, "Come on. Five minutes are up."

"They're alright. Still at the hospital. Keeping them for a week at least until they know the baby will be fine. Miranda is good." Nash harrumphed. "She's going mad not knowing where you are."

Silence hung in the air like stalactites on a cave ceiling. They both knew what had to be done but Nash was not happy about it. "I'll tell her."

"Thanks, Nash."

"You owe me big time."

Nash heard men on the other end waiting for the phone taunting Hank. "Come on. You're not the only one here."

"Gotta go."

The line went dead. Nash sat on the stool by the phone, put his head in his hands and let out a huge sigh. How did he get himself in this stupid mess anyway? This is why he liked living the loner life of a cowboy. You were responsible for you and that's it. And the animals. But that was it. He longed for the mountains and wide-open spaces.

Nash dialed his boss's number. Walt Davis had been his boss since he worked on the ranch in Wyoming with Hank a few years ago. Walt was an old school cowboy with a strong work ethic. Nash highly respected him and he'd been like a father to both Nash and Hank. Didn't know if he'd answer the barn phone but it was feeding time. He'd try.

"Hlo…" He answered on the first ring.

"Walt?'"

"Speakin."

"Walt…Nash. I need a favor. Hank's in jail and he's a mess. Could you go to his hearing? I'm still helping his wife out with the horses at their farm."

He exhaled loudly. "Jail? What'd our boy do?"

"Member that dude at the bar he got in a fight with couple years ago?"

"Thought that got sorted."

"Hank did too. But he left town before he finished his probation. Can you go?"

"You bet. Anything to help another cowboy." Both men of few words, they hung up after Nash shared the hearing details.

Nash went about shoving piles of manure in the stalls. He worked out his anger on the pitchfork, dumping his frustrations with every forkful plopped into the wheelbarrow. He'd figure it out. Figure out a way to tell Miranda the real story about her husband. Shove. Plop. Shove. Plop.

Hank owed him big time. Shove. Plop. Shove. Plop. The barn wall sang out as the phone rang. Again. Nash wiped sweat from his brow and watched a calico cat as it scurried across the cement after a mouse and disappeared behind the bales of hay. He continued shoveling.

He ignored the phone. But it kept ringing and ringing, piercing through the solitude he'd hoped for. He knew the only way to stop the noise was to answer it. He trotted to the wall and picked up the receiver. He slammed it down. It started to ring again. He bent to yank the phone line out of the wall and reached toward the cord when he stopped. It could be Miranda. He didn't want to be a jerk. She didn't need another man letting her down. Such a good person. Hank didn't deserve her.

He picked up the receiver. "Graaf residence." His deep voice rumbled into the phone like a bass drum.

"Hi. Is Tanya there?" A flash of electricity careened through his tall body, bronzed from ranch work. He recognized Tanya's boyfriend's needy, controlling voice.

One of Nash's long legs hooked a boot in front of the other and he leaned his back into the wall. "No. She's not."

"Where is she?"

Nash couldn't believe Tanya liked this guy. He got on Nash's nerves. Daniel seemed like the kind of guy that had to always have a thumb on his girlfriend's comings and goings. He didn't know how Tanya could breathe. Nash snapped, "How should I know?"

Daniel sounded like a creaky barn window, flapping in the wind. "Could you give her a message for me?"

Nash didn't want to do anything for Daniel. Especially the mood he was in. He was done being the go-between. But especially the likes of Daniel. Tanya was another woman who deserved more than the man she was with.

"You still there?"

"Yep."

"Nash. Is it?"

"Yep."

"Well." Daniel's voice twisted into a snarl. "Can you tell her something for me?"

"I don't know where she is. Not my job."

"She's still working there, isn't she? I mean helping the Graafs'."

"Far as I know." Nash knew Tanya, Miranda's best friend since childhood, was probably at the hospital or at Miranda and Hank's house.

"Tell Tanya her coach is giving her two days to get back to Colorado."

"He can tell her himself."

Daniel's voice tried to convey command, but Nash knew Daniel was an insecure bully using his muscles and athletic body to dominate his way through life. He knew the kind. Boyfriends that tried to control their girlfriends.

"Can't seem to find her. So, her coach got a hold of me."

Nash wondered what all that was about or if it was even true. He didn't want Tanya to miss out on the 1988 Seoul Olympics in September. She was an amazing gymnast and had worked her whole life for this moment. He'd seen her doing flips in the yard. But Nash was suspicious of Daniel. Didn't trust him further than the short hair on his head.

With gruffness in his voice, he said, "If I see her, I'll give her the message."

Daniel started to say something else. Nash hung up. He rested his hand on the receiver. What was he? A secretary? He shook his head and got back to work.

CHAPTER TWO

Miranda's body felt like she'd been through a war, yet she was exhilarated as she fixed her gaze on the beautiful baby sleeping on her chest. She caressed her small head and softly murmured. "Hello Emily." The newborn nestled into her mother's breast and began nursing. Luckily, they'd been given a private room. The door was shut, and it was quiet. Peaceful as if nothing was going on except for the miracle of a newborn coming into the world. But Miranda couldn't shake the thread of anxiety pivoting inside her brain all the way to the tips of her toes. Where was her husband, Hank? Her tall, brawny husband wasn't there. She needed to look into his sea green eyes and cherish this moment with him.

Her mother and her best friend stood on either side of the bed and admired the newborn. Only moments before she had been born.

Through tears, Justine touched Emily's damp hair and said, "She's beautiful, Miranda."

Tanya blew her nose. "You're a *mom*, Ran. You did a great job."

Her eyes shot upward and through a weak and tired voice, Miranda said, "Where's Hank?"

Tanya and Justine looked at each other.

Tanya shrugged. "Miranda, you and little Emily rest for a minute. Your mom and I will go see what's up."

Miranda drifted off to sleep just as a nurse with an angelic face came in to attend to the baby and mom.

Tanya whispered to the nurse. "We're leaving for a little bit. Take care of those two. We'll be right outside if you need us."

The nurse smiled. "Why don't you take a break and go get something to eat?"

Tanya grabbed Justine's hand, and they rushed out of the room.

In the hallway, the waiting area was empty and only one man occupied a chair. Tanya led Justine to a couple of brown Scandinavian style armchairs with high backs in the corner of the waiting room.

With anxious eyes, Justine said, "*Where* is Hank?" She curved her platinum blond bob around her ears.

Tanya took a big breath and sighed. "Don't freak, Mrs. Graaf."

Justine twisted her hands together.

They both watched as two nurses and a doctor rushed into a room next to Miranda's.

Jutine put her hand on Tanya's arm and squeezed. "Tell me."

"Hank is in jail." She expelled her words on a whisper. "In Wyoming."

Justine's face paled. "What!" She put her hand to her mouth and the other on the wooden armrest as she tried to get her bearings.

"Code blue. Room 412. Code blue." The doctor and one nurse came out of the room next to Miranda and rushed down the hallway, their white medical shoes squeaking on the linoleum as they ran.

"Hank had some legal stuff he hadn't sorted when he lived in Wyoming a couple years ago." Tanya let that sink in for a couple moments. "He had a warrant out for his arrest."

"Why wouldn't he take care of it? Justine's trembling hand swiped her face. "And. Why didn't he tell Miranda?"

Tanya shrugged. She looked around and realized Nash had gone. Her lips twisted. "Wimp," she mumbled.

Just then, Justine's fiancé, Richard, walked over, his perfect white smile contrasting his tanning booth tan, coffee in each hand. "Congratulations, grandma." He gave each of them a cup and bent to kiss Justine.

His expensive cologne filled her nostrils, usually sparking heat within her but today its spicy scent triggered a slight headache.

"There's cream and sugar in one and the other just cream, like you like it, Justine."

She flashed him with half a smile "Thanks."

His forehead wrinkled. "I thought you'd be more excited. Is Miranda, ok?"

Justine breathed in and exhaled audibly as she gave Richard a side eye. "Hank's in jail."

His mouth dropped and he lowered himself onto a nearby chair. "What happened?"

She pressed her thighs together, running her hands along her long legs. "We're trying to figure that out."

"Does Miranda know?"

Justine sucked in a breath and put a hand to her mouth. "What are we going to tell her? She'll be devastated."

Silence swirled around the three of them as they stared into space.

The angelic nurse came out of Miranda's room and walked up to the group. "Miranda is asking about her husband. I don't know what to tell her." Her eyebrows lifted. "So maybe one of you could go talk to her."

Tanya sighed. "We'd better get this over with. Miranda's got to know."

Justine stood. Her face was deadpan serious. "Richard. You might as well go home." She leaned in and gave him a peck on the cheek.

His face crumpled. "I'll wait."

Justine shrugged. "Suit yourself. But I'm going to stay a while."

In a sulky voice he said, "How'll you get home?"

As she left the waiting room, she said, "I'll catch a cab."

Once inside Miranda's room, they each took a chair and scooted up to the side of the hospital bed. Emily slept in a bassinet at the end of the bed, her soft breathing filled the air with a calm interlude before the harsh storm of what Miranda was about to hear.

Tanya started in. "Ran. We need to tell you something."

Miranda scooched herself upward and leaned back on the pillows stacked behind her. She stared at Tanya with a blank face. "Something's wrong with Hank?"

Tanya glanced at Justine. "Sort of."

"Just tell me."

Justine took Miranda's hand. She blurted. "Hank's in jail."

Miranda's eyes bugged. "He's what?"

Emily let out a cry and then fell back asleep.

As Tanya relayed the story of Hank being picked up by the Wyoming police and transported to Cheyenne, Miranda's face got redder and redder. "I can't believe he would do this to us." Her whole body was tired, sore, and she needed rest. But with the news of Hank, she could feel the spark of fire flashing through her.

Tanya said, "Do you want to see if we can get a hold of him so you can at least talk to him?"

Miranda spit out her anger. "Yeah. So, I can yell at him." She put her head in her hands. "What am I going to do?" She couldn't believe this was happening. How could the man she loved, her husband, now the father of their baby, miss his daughter's birth?

Tanya and Justine wrapped their arms around her and let her cry.

Finally, Justine lifted Miranda's chin and looked into her eyes. "Honey, you are going to take care of that beautiful baby and we're going to help you. Together we'll get through this."

Miranda sniffled. "Thanks, Mom." She wiped her nose with the back of her hand.

Tanya reached over and lifted a box of Kleenex off the side table and handed it to Miranda.

She blew her nose. "Thanks you guys for being here. I couldn't have done it without you."

Justine smiled. "Wouldn't have missed it. But that baby was coming whether we were here or not."

Tanya didn't know how her friend would survive this, but she knew she would somehow. Miranda was a strong woman. She'd figure out a way. Darn that Hank, anyway.

The nurse settled Miranda into a private hospital room: a bathroom, two well-worn visitor chairs against a wall, a metal IV stand with a saline bag and a pressure cuff next to the bed and a rolling table and a nightstand stationed near a window. Justine scooted one of the chairs next to the bed and said to Tanya, "Why don't you go get something to eat, honey? I'll sit with her."

Tanya felt like she could use a break from all the drama. There was one thing she needed to do before she went to the cafeteria. She smiled at Justine. "Thanks. I'll be back in a little bit. Need anything?"

Justine shook her head. "Tell Richard he can go on home. I'll call him later."

Miranda fisted her hands on either side of her body, trying to get comfortable in the hospital bed. "Tonny?"

"Yeah, Ran?"

"Could you call the vet that's supposed to take care of my practice until I'm back? Thought I had another month. Dr. Gerrit De Van. Should be in the phone book. He's in Clinton."

"Of course." Tanya left the room and went looking for a pay phone.

CHAPTER THREE

In the visitor lounge Tanya made a call to Dr. De Van. Then she slipped a couple more dimes in the pay phone and called the barn at the Graafs'. She figured Nash had chickened out wanting to be in a familiar turf, like a barn filled with horses.

The phone kept ringing and ringing. Tanya was about to give up when Nash answered. "What do you want *now*?"

She let out a laugh. "Wow. Someone's cranky."

"Oh." He sighed. "Sorry Tanya."

"You took off before the miracle happened."

"I waited until the baby was born."

"Why didn't you wait and see the baby?"

"I didn't think it would be a good idea for me to see her, Hank not being there and all." As he was telling her what happened, the warmth and soothing tone of his voice tapped into the visceral part of her body.

"About that." Tanya leaned back, her foot against the hospital wall. "What's happening with Hank?" She stared at a patient moaning, attendants pushing her on a gurney as they passed.

All the chaos of the last several hours: Nash and Tanya rushing Miranda to the hospital when she went into labor, staying by Miranda's side when Emily was born, and keeping Hank's whereabouts a secret had been a lot for Tanya. Hearing

Nash's velvety bass voice, Tanya's muscles released the tension they'd been holding on to. She had never been around babies and had never known a pregnant woman before Miranda. So, experiencing this special moment in her best friend's life with a man she'd only known a couple of weeks bonded her to Nash in a way she'd never known before.

Nash had that cowboy way about him and gave Tanya something to hold onto. A quiet, calming effect, that let her know everything was going to be ok. She wondered if he was just built that way or if he'd learned how to calm those around him working with cattle and horses. Tanya imagined Nash wrapping his arms around her, allowing the calming effect to go even deeper as she melted into him.

Nash continued, "He called me from jail. Waiting for sentencing. Who knows what'll happen next."

"I hear ya. Hank needs to get home and be a dad. Miranda's not too happy." She wrapped the cord around her finger. "Thanks for filling in."

"The least I can do."

"I'm going to stay at Miranda and Hank's house for a couple days. I can help you when I get to the farm." Tanya pictured their newly built ranch style home positioned next to Miranda's new veterinarian practice, that adjoined the barn, a door separating the two. Hank had surprised Miranda with the new build only a few months prior when she returned from her internship in England.

"That'd be great. I could use help with the horses. Maybe exercise them."

"We could take them out for a ride."

"You ride?"

"Heck, yeah. Miranda and I rode as kids for years." She smiled a little as she reminisced the two of them exploring the rows of tall corn, riding bareback in the late summer evenings, as cicadas buzzed their loud chorus while the sun went down.

The memory melted tension and lowered her shoulders if only for an instant.

"Really?"

"Rocko's my guy."

"He's a gentle one. Mandy bosses him."

"And he just takes it and follows her around."

"Well. I'd better get to it."

"I'll see you soon."

"Oh. And Tanya?"

"Yeah?"

"Daniel called. He didn't sound so happy."

Tanya flinched. She pictured Daniel's tall sprinter leg muscles twitching as he jumped up and down warming up at the starting blocks during a meet preparing for the Olympic games. She knew her boyfriend would be furious at the idea of her helping at the farm and especially exercising the horses on a trail ride. Especially, the trail ride. "What'd he say?"

"Said your coach wanted you back."

"Thanks for the update."

"You bet." Nash paused. His voice became quiet, with the bass lowering to a soft timbre. "See ya Tanya."

CHAPTER FOUR

Later that same day, in Miranda's hospital room, she awoke from her nap with a startle. She sat upright in her bed. "Where's Emily?"

Justine, sitting in a chair next to the bed, placed her hand on Miranda's leg. "She's in the nursery, dear."

"I want her here with me." Miranda started to take rapid shallow breaths as if she couldn't get enough air. "Now," she said in a weak voice, barely audible.

Justine had never seen her daughter unhinged. Sad, when Stanley, her husband and Miranda's father, had died. Yes. Angry at times. But never so out of control with her emotions. It was like Miranda had met her maximum stress level with Hank in jail and not able to provide her with the support a new mom should have from her husband.

Justine popped up from her chair and slapped the call button.

Within minutes a nurse scooted into the room. "What can I help you with?"

"My daughter is having a panic attack. She wants her baby with her in the room. Could you bring a crib in here so she can stay with her?"

"I'll have to check with the doctor. He wanted us to keep an eye on Emily, since she was born early." She turned to leave. "I'll be back shortly."

Miranda started trembling and a trickle of sweat rolled down her neck and chest. Justine leaned inward and Miranda grabbed her mother's arm. Justine said, "It'll be ok, honey. Take slow breaths. Breathe with me. Look at me."

Miranda stared into the void, dead-eyed and detached as if she'd left the room.

"That's it." Justine knew she needed to help Miranda relax. She said in the calmest voice she could muster, "Slow down." Justine purposefully breathed slowly and deeply. "Breathe." Miranda held on tightly, her nails digging into Justine's forearm.

Just then, the door opened. Justine said, "Bout time. Our girl here is having a hard time."

"Hi ladies." Justine swung her head around to find Richard popping into the room. "How's everyone doing?"

Justine opened her mouth to say something, then thought better of it. She felt her jaw tense.

Ricard bent to kiss Justine on the cheek. "How's our new mamma?"

Miranda continued panting. Her face turned red as she began to cry. "I… want…my…baby…," she said between breaths.

Words fell out of Justine's mouth. "Read the room, Richard."

He jerked back. "Everything ok?"

Justine *tsked*. How could he not see that her daughter was having a hard time? All because of Hank. What should have been a beautiful moment in Miranda's life, and for all of them, was hindered by Hank's stupidity. She thought Hank was better than that. How could he be so thoughtless? Keeping his legal issues secret made things worse in the long run. And here they were, Hank creating distress for his new family. She never realized Hank was that selfish. Justine ground her teeth.

Richard sat in a chair at the edge of the room. "Have you talked to Hank yet?"

Justine glared at him.

Miranda started breathing faster.

Justine thought Miranda might faint if she kept it up. "I'm going out to see what's taking that nurse so long." She flashed a look at Richard. "Sit with her. Breathe with her and have her take slow, deep breaths." Justine scooted out of the room.

In the hallway, Justine looked around for the nurse that had left the room earlier. She went up to the nurses' station and leaned in. She said, "Excuse me."

A woman was busy clicking keys on a typewriter. The woman ignored her as Justine tapped her fingernails on the counter.

"Excuse me. My daughter, Miranda Graaf, is having a rough go of it." She motioned toward Miranda's room. "Could you send someone down?" Her lips pursed. Justine snapped, "Immediately."

The typist gestured with one finger. "Wait just a moment please."

"I won't wait a moment. Do something. Now."

The typist looked up, shot Justine a nasty glare, picked up the phone and summoned a nurse. She nodded her head as she listened to the other line. "Ok, I see. I'll tell her." She looked at Justine, blinked slowly and cocked her head. "Someone is on their way." She sighed and then continued typing.

Justine pivoted. "I've got to get back to Miranda." She ran down the hallway to her daughter's room.

Once back, Justine pressed a palm to her heart as she saw a nurse handing Emily to Miranda. She sat at Miranda's side and began instructing Miranda on how to feed her baby. Miranda seemed calmer and happier now that her baby was with her. After a few minutes, the nurse smiled and said, as she gestured, "The call button is right there if you need anything." And then left the room.

Richard sat in the corner, looking like he'd like to disappear. Justine went over to him, sat beside him, putting a hand on his knee. "Go home, Richard. I'm staying here tonight."

"I can keep you company."

"I think it's best if it's just me."

A slight pout spread over his face. "Don't you want me here? I could get you food and coffee and bring it back to the room."

All the stress of supporting Miranda while giving birth to Emily the previous night, and the shock in the morning, finding out that Hank was in jail had taken its toll on Justine. She didn't want to have to take care of Richard too, and she knew if he stayed, she'd be worried about his feelings. Her voice snapped, "Thanks for the offer, but we'll be ok."

Richard rose and stood at the edge of the room looking at Justine and Miranda and then back at Justine again like he was lost and searching for a place to land.

Justine felt bad that she didn't want Richard there, but she just couldn't handle his neediness and clueless behavior. Miranda needed her mother. And she didn't have the energy to focus on Richard right then. He'd have to deal with it. "Honey, why don't you go to the farm and spend the night there? Tomorrow morning you can get some goodies at the bakery a couple blocks down the street from the hospital before you come and see us." Justine got up, grabbed his coat from the chair he'd been sitting in and went to Richard, kissing him on the cheek. She handed him the coat. "See you tomorrow, Richard."

He hesitated and then looked at Miranda. "Congratulations. Emily is a beautiful baby." He turned to leave and then turned back. "It'll all work out with Hank." And then he left.

Justine groaned inside. Richard could be thoughtful. She knew that. But he could also be so irritating and old fashioned in his views and wanting women to be taken care of. And at the same time, he expected a woman to cater to his needs as well. She didn't know if he could understand and see that

Justine and Miranda were two strong women that could handle things even if at the moment it didn't look like it.

Yet, it was nice to have someone thoughtful like Richard. She felt guilty and even a little bit sad that she hadn't included Richard in the birth of Miranda's baby. She'd certainly kept him at bay, for sure.

And as she watched Miranda snuggle Emily, she realized that her sadness was mostly because Stanley wasn't there to share in this moment. However, she felt his spirit nearby, in this room with them. Was that why she kept Richard at arm's length? She didn't want to include him because it would taint their family, the three of them that was her past. This was blood. Emily was both from Stanley and from Justine's family. Richard was like a substitute grandpa. It just wasn't the same.

Justine sat in a chair at the edge of the room watching Miranda feed her baby. The nurse had been very patient and understanding with Miranda while she learned how to be a mom for the first time. Justine leaned back and closed her eyes taking a break. She thought about how Richard could play a role in this family and how she could try to be more understanding and allow him to fall into the role of grandpa.

But did she want to?

After several minutes and a quick nap, Justine went over to the bed where Emily was sleeping on Miranda's chest, swaddled in a pink blanket. Miranda was fast asleep as well. Justine bent and gently cradled the baby in her arms and sat in a chair beside the bed. She kissed Emily gently on the top of her head, thick blond curly hair framing her angelic face. Justine sat back and looked at the little being sleeping, and a sense of wonderment ran through her at the miracle that was her granddaughter.

CHAPTER FIVE

Back in the Cheyenne, Wyoming jail, Hank slouched on his bunk bed, dressed in the distinctive orange inmate uniform, the same as the three other men in his cell. He ran a hand over his shaved head and stared straight ahead at the gray cement block wall. The room smelled like a men's locker room after a football game: body odor, dirty uniforms, strong disinfectants and industrial cleaning products.

The big burly guy on the upper bunk across the room glared at him. His caustic voice misted spittle as he said, "What're you looking at?" The muscles on his tattooed arm rippled as he made a fist.

Hank glanced at the guy. That was the real question, wasn't it? He was here because he made some stupid choices. The anger Hank felt rang deep in his bones and a fine coat of numbness dusted over him, shutting out any fear. The guy in front of him didn't scare him.

If Hank had told Miranda in the first place… And if he had made sure that everything had been taken care of before he left Wyoming two years prior, all of this would never have happened. He had spent a couple days in jail once before when he'd gotten arrested for punching that guy in the bar two years before. He knew better than to mess with the law.

How could he have been so careless? He had missed the birth of his first born. He swallowed the acid in his throat.

At the preliminary hearing his attorney warned him he may get two to three months probation and community service. If Hank couldn't be with his family for several weeks it would seem like forever. He put his head in his hands. He'd have to wait for the sentencing and see what the judge ordered.

When Hank didn't respond, the guy on the bunk threw a shoe at him. "What're you in for?"

Hank slowly looked at him. If Hank's eyes could turn into flames, they'd burn holes into the bunk in front of him. "I punched a guy." Hank knew he'd better get along with the rest of the inmates or he'd make it harder on himself. He'd learned even in the short time he had been in jail two years before there was a pecking order. He shoved his chin outward. "You?"

"I beat up my wife." He shrugged. "At least that's what the neighbors said. I was just teaching her a lesson. She's always yammering at me." He smirked. "She deserved it."

He could hear shouting and clanging against the bars nearby. Hank had to pretend to be someone else and act the part of criminal while he was there. Otherwise, if he acted better than others, he'd get beaten up. It was a rough place to take up space. Hank didn't know if he had it in him to act and put on a show. He'd screwed up and he had to figure out a way to get what he had back again. To make it up to Miranda. And his baby daughter. Emily wouldn't know any difference now. But what would she think of her dad when she heard the story later in life? Would she think her dad was a screw up? Hank wanted his family to respect him.

He wanted to be different than his own father who had left his family when Hank was a kid. He hated him for that and had no respect for his father and hadn't seen him in years. He didn't know if he was alive or not and didn't care. He didn't want Emily to think of him that way. She couldn't. Hank would have to think of a way to make it up to Miranda, the love of his life, and be a dad that his daughter could look up to and be proud of.

"Hey, don't be rude. I'm talking." The burly guy must have been six feet tall and had a scar that ran diagonally across his cheek and down his chin. His fingernails were black with dirt and the guy looked like he hadn't bathed in weeks. He reminded Hank of an ally cat that had been around the block a few too many times, getting into fights and sleeping and eating wherever it could. Hank didn't want to get on the bad side of this guy.

Hank shoved the thoughts of his family aside and tried to play the role of watching his back as an inmate.

The guy jumped down off his bunk and came up to Hank within a few inches. "You pay attention and do what I say, and we'll get along just fine."

Hank grimaced, twitching his jaw muscles. He thought treating a woman like this guy had was criminal and he should be punished for abusing his wife. Hank knew if he didn't stand up to this guy now, he'd lose respect, and even though jail wasn't as rough as prison, he'd still have to watch his back. He leaned in, stood his ground and realized he was the same height as this joker. He was a bully trying to muscle his way through his time here, and probably everywhere in life.

Hank nudged his chin upward, puffed his chest and flexed his hands into fists and the guy backed away, retreating to his bunk.

Just then, a worker pushed a cart delivering food to each pod. He knocked on the door and hollered, "Lunch."

Each of the guys retreated off their bunk and grabbed a tray and brought it back to their beds. The smell of institutional food swirled inside their cell. Hank looked at the chipped beef, creamed corn and mashed potatoes on the tray in his lap. He took a bite of his roll which was dry and flopped it back down.

He was going to lose weight while he was there, for sure. He wasn't hungry anyway. He plopped the tray at the edge of the door to the cell, went back to his bed, stretched out and closed his eyes. He'd make it through this somehow.

CHAPTER SIX

A few days after Miranda gave birth to Emily, Tanya woke up and opened her eyes. For a moment she'd forgotten where she was. She looked around the room, a light yellow on the walls and pastel shades of mint green, pink and yellow on the gingham comforter tucked underneath her chin on a twin size bed. The sun shone through a crack in the blind on the window, and Tanya remembered she was staying at Miranda and Hank's house, sleeping in Emily's room. A crib stood in the corner and a changing table next to a white dresser. Pretty pink and yellow baby outfits hung in the closet, ready to be worn once Emily had grown to fit them.

Miranda, fifteen miles from the farm, still recovering at St Luke's hospital that perched on a bluff overlooking downtown Davenport. Hank, eight hundred miles away, locked in a jail cell. Tanya had promised she would stay until Miranda could bring the baby home.

Tanya was lucky that her gymnastics coach in Colorado believed in time off and that it was important to have recovery time. Even so, Tanya had to get back to training for the Olympics. She had almost forgotten her Olympic dream lately with all the drama of babies being born early, husbands going to jail, and boyfriends getting jealous of cute cowboys.

That cute cowboy slept out in the barn last night. Probably lying on bales of hay, saddle for a pillow, and his body covered in a horse blanket. She'd try to talk him into coming into the house. At least sleep in a comfortable bed instead. He'd said he was used to sleeping in the rough outdoors when driving cattle, and barn floors when waiting for a mare to foal.

It was probably just as well that Nash slept in the barn because when she thought about his rippled chest, glimpsed as he was changing shirts after mucking stalls, and the deep glow in his gray eyes when he looked at her, Tanya didn't trust herself. She couldn't guarantee that she would keep to herself. Her pulse surged when he appeared, and her heart danced when he looked at her. What those feelings were all about she didn't know. What she did know was that she was committed to Daniel. They had common dreams as athletes and he understood the hard work it took to be an Olympian.

She didn't know what Nash's dreams were. He just seemed like a regular guy, no drama, a guy who knew what he wanted and was sure of himself without being garish or full of himself. Nash exuded a calm, confident energy.

And he attracted her so much it made her crazy.

A good guy. Moral character. Respected women. A gentle soul. A rugged cowboy, weathered from the mountain air and hard work. And not awful looking either. Nash heated her body way beyond 98.6, that's for sure.

She realized Daniel was none of those things except he was a hard worker. He was focused and rode on the train of his path to the Olympics, aiming for golds in the 110- and 400-meter hurdles. She loved that about him. So devoted and disciplined. His sprinter body was lean and ripped.

What was she going to do? She got up from bed, put her jeans and t-shirt on. Miranda's German Shepard, Ben, rose from the floor. She'd forgotten he was there, and she almost tripped over him. She rubbed the dog's soft black and tan head. "Hey, buddy." He licked her hand, and he followed Tanya into the bathroom, where she ran cold water over her face. The timer on the coffee maker in the kitchen turned on and the aroma of hot caffeine filled the air.

She slipped on a pair of Miranda's cowboy boots, put on her jean jacket and grabbed a mug of coffee on her way out to the barn. She thought about what chores she'd do once she slid that barn door open. The horses needed to be groomed. The barn cats needed to be fed. She could call back Miranda's veterinarian patients that had tried to get a hold of her.

And she could stay as far away from the sexy cowboy in the barn, as far as possible. She walked up to the wooden door and stopped. She took a deep breath, talking low to herself. *Just be cool. Be cool. You're an athlete. You know how to focus. Just do what you need to do for Miranda.*

Tanya slowly slid open the door and peeked inside. A fluffy yellow barn cat slid through the opening and walked a figure eight around her legs, purring. She bent to pet his soft fur and suddenly wished she could hide out in Miranda's office and take Ben and the cats and just hang out, disappearing from the world. She felt the pressure Daniel put on her to be a gold medalist, to be a good girlfriend, and the pressure from her coach to win in her sport. She knew this was part of it, the life of a high-level gymnast. It wasn't for the meek. And suddenly, she felt the pressure of Miranda's drama coming down on her as well. She wanted to help her best friend and the baby, but Hank had really put a burden on all of them. His absence loomed heavy and affected them all. Tanya would be on her way back to Colorado if Hank wasn't in jail. Miranda wouldn't need her. Justine was there for Miranda and Hank would have taken care of the farm.

But now everything had changed because he had made one stupid mistake and landed in jail. She hoped Hank realized how much his choices had made things hard for all of them, mostly for Miranda and Emily.

Tanya stepped inside the barn, the yellow cat following close behind. She made her way into the tack room. Her nose breathed in the earthy scent of leather and she grabbed a pail and gathered a curry comb, dandy brush, and hoof pick. As she pivoted, heading toward Mandy's stall, she ran head-on into Nash. She felt her face flush. He was so hot. How would she get through her work without falling to her knees, crumbling from the attraction she felt?

The shadow on his face from his black Stetson added to the mystery and intrigue of her wanting to know him better. Who was this guy? And what made him tick? Tanya had a flash of them hanging out in the barn, stretched out in the bales of straw, talking, laughing and their faces closing in for a kiss. What was she doing? *Stop it*, she told herself. *Enough. You are with Daniel.* She shook her head slightly as if to clear off the sizzling energy trapped inside her body.

His eyes widened, and she felt his breath quicken. They were that close. "Tanya?"

Her legs weakened and she squeaked out, "Hi, Nash." The yellow cat jumped up on a saddle and rubbed his head against her arm.

Nash's bass voice drummed a beat throughout her body. "What are you doing here?"

She tipped her head to the side. "What do you mean?" She *tsked*, trying to sound sure of herself, even though her insides were mush. "Miranda had her baby early, remember? I'm here to help. Just like you are." Tanya stepped around Nash, and her shoulder brushed his arm as she passed him, walking out the tack room door and into the main barn. Heat, and what felt like shreds of sparkling tinsel on a Christmas tree, cascaded throughout her belly. "Thanks to your screwball friend, Hank. We're all filling in the gaps."

"He's caused an avalanche of problems," Nash said behind her.

She pivoted to face him. Nash's deep buttery voice and the tone in which he sympathized how difficult things had been touched something inside that no one else had understood. Hearing his voice calmed her and soothed the restlessness she felt from the shaky relationship with Daniel, the anger she felt at Hank and the worry she felt about making it to the Olympics. Until Nash spoke these words, she hadn't realized how difficult the last few months had been. She'd pushed the anxiety, the fear, the insecurities down, down deeply and hadn't thought or felt any of it, until now. A tear trickled down her cheek and landed in the bucket she was holding. She quickly swiped away the wetness on her face, hoping Nash hadn't seen her emotions spilling out. This revelation overwhelmed the strong disciplined athlete inside and tears kept coming. She turned away, not wanting Nash to see the vulnerable side of her.

Out of the corner of her eye she saw Nash reach his hand out.

She shook her head and rubbed her eyes.

"It's ok you know. What they're needing us to do for them is a lot."

He put his hand on her shoulder. "I can't imagine how hard this must be, watching your best friend do this without her husband."

It just made Tanya cry even harder.

"Come over here." Nash led her to a bench in front of Rocko's stall. "Have a seat."

He went into the bathroom and came out with a roll of toilet paper and handed it to her. "I couldn't find any Kleenex. That'll have to do."

She cracked a slight smile. "Thanks." She wound off a long strip of paper and then blew her nose. "That was unexpected. Sorry."

He sat down beside her, quietly, and waited for her to talk. But she sensed that if she decided not to tell him anything it would be ok with him. He didn't seem like a guy that needed to know all the answers to questions. He was just a calming presence. And that was what she needed now. No demands from her. No one to tell her what to do.

She needed someone that would just be with her and help her feel less alone. Because right now, she didn't have anyone she could lean on. Miranda was preoccupied, understandably. Tanya's mom was never there for her. It was always the other way around. And Daniel was someone who always had the answers. His answers. His solution, no matter if it didn't coincide with what Tanya wanted or needed. He would listen but then tell her what to do. And her friends, if you could call them that, on her gymnastics team were so competitive. They wouldn't tolerate weakness or vulnerability. Plus, she never knew who she could trust. There was a lot of back-stabbing in the sport, especially at Tanya's level of competition.

Tanya and Nash just sat in the quiet listening to the horses munch on their breakfast, the yellow cat chasing mice and the sound of sparrows fluttering about in the rafters. The last time Tanya had felt this at peace was when she rode Rocko before Miranda had left for England for her internship with Dr. James Herriot in Yorkshire. She began feeling a little lighter. Yep. Things would get better. She'd figure a way to do it all. She glanced at Nash. "Thanks. Means a lot you just sitting with me."

He looked at her and his clear gray eyes were filled with hope. "Seems you needed just to be."

"How'd you get so smart?"

"It's what I get when I'm riding the range. Peace and quiet."

"That one with the horses and cattle kind of thing?"

He cracked a smile, lighting Tanya up with his bright warmth that radiated through her and around her.

"Something like that."

Just then the barn phone started to ring. And just like that their bubble was broken.

Nash slowly meandered over to the phone hanging on the wall. He picked up the black receiver. "Graaf residence, Nash here." He tilted his head. "Yep. Right here." He stretched the long cord as he walked toward Tanya. He handed her the handset. "Daniel's askin for ya."

Tanya swiped her hands over her face, sucked in a big breath of air and stood. Nash's hand brushed hers as she wrapped her hand around the receiver. He strode to the back of the barn.

She braced herself for Daniel complaining about the fact that she was still there, still helping Miranda, and that Nash was there too. "Hi, babe."

Tanya could sense the tension in Daniel's voice even before he talked. And it was all because Nash was there with her. She suddenly felt weary of his jealousy and possessiveness. He didn't have anything to worry about. Tanya loved Daniel. Just because her body was reacting with unfounded sensations, and she felt her temperature rise when she was around Nash didn't mean that she had feelings for him. Nash was a good-looking guy. Why wouldn't she react that way? Who wouldn't? There would be something wrong with her if she didn't get flustered when she was around him. There, that was settled then. She was a normal female human being, just reacting to a good-looking guy.

"Daniel, are you still there?"

"Yeah, sorry babe. How's Miranda and the baby?"

She held the receiver away from her ear and looked at it. *Who was this guy, and where did my boyfriend go?* "She's doing good. They're staying in the hospital a week just to make sure things are ok since Emily was born a month early."

Tanya had called Daniel the evening that Emily was born. She'd caught him up to speed about the birth and about Hank going to jail in Wyoming. At the time, all Daniel could say about the situation was that Hank was an idiot. And that it wasn't fair for them to ask her to help when she was training for the Olympics. Daniel never asked about Miranda or Emily. He complained and never once said he understood what she had to do for her friend.

One of the challenging pieces of their relationship was that Daniel always made it about him even though the words sounded like they were about Tanya and his concern for her making it big in the Olympics. Tanya could read between the lines. It was really about the inconvenience of her being away from him. And that he was insecure when she was away from him. Well, he'd just have to deal with it. Tanya was going to do what she had to do. She could train there in Davenport, Iowa. She didn't have to be in Colorado yet. She'd do both, help her best friend and make it to the Olympics. And. Win. Gold. Tanya flipped her ponytail between her fingers. She'd show him. And the entire world. She could do it.

"Thanks for asking about Miranda and the baby. I really appreciate it."

"I care about them. Hank is a real jerk for being in jail." Daniel exhaled. "What an idiot."

"You said that already."

"He should be there for his family."

"Agreed."

"How long do you think you'll be there?"

Tanya rolled her eyes and looked upward. "As long as it takes."

Silence on the other end. And then, "And how long will the cowboy be staying?"

And there it was.

She took a deep breath in. She closed her eyes. Then slow exhale. "I don't know, Daniel. He didn't tell ---"

He cut her off. "Maybe I should take the weekend to fly in. To help I mean."

"You hate the country." She half-laughed. "Mucking stalls isn't your jam."

"I'd come and help if it meant you'd get back to training sooner."

Tanya knew it was only because Daniel wanted to keep an eye on Nash and her.

"Thanks, babe. I got it." Before he had time to get into the reasons why she should leave or why Daniel should come there, she wrapped up the phone call. "I'd better go. I've got work to do. I'll call you later. Love ya."

Tanya hung up the phone. She stood scanning the barn. Nash had disappeared. She did have a lot of work to do, and she'd start by grooming Mandy, the thing she wanted to do when she came into the barn a half hour earlier.

She grabbed a halter and lead rope from a hook on the wall and headed toward Mandy's stall. Maybe she could get a run in this afternoon and do some stretching and practice dance moves for her floor routine that evening. She'd make them both work, maintaining her gymnast fitness and helping on the farm.

CHAPTER SEVEN

Nash had disappeared as soon as Tanya started talking to Daniel. What a putz. Tanya deserved better. A guy that gave her respect. Someone that was strong and treated her well. Maybe Daniel was a good athlete and maybe he would win a gold in the upcoming Olympics, but he knew nothing about how to treat a girlfriend. He was so insecure when Tanya came to Iowa. Who knows what he was like in Colorado at training camp? He probably tried to control Tanya there too. And Tanya was a woman who had her own thoughts and opinions.

Nash threw some straw in the stalls of the horses and his mind wandered, thinking about how he had wanted to put his arm around Tanya when they sat there in the quiet as she cried. She was attractive, *really* attractive. Her compact, powerful frame and her pretty smile and chocolate eyes made him breathless. But he wasn't *that* kind of guy that would home in on someone else's girlfriend. He felt a real connection to her, more than he'd ever felt with a woman. He'd only talked with her a few times since they'd met at the Graaf's six months prior. When Nash had picked up Hank to go buy Quarter Horses and they were introduced Nash felt a spark then. He'd dated, sure, but nobody ever stood out. At least not until he met Tanya. So, he'd have to wait and see how things turned out with Tanya and Daniel. He hoped she'd come to her senses and dump the guy. Nash just wanted what was best for her, as long as it was someone who treated her right.

He finished cleaning the stalls and went outside to take a walk, hoping the cool spring air would clear his head, spotting the flock of red-winged blackbirds overhead. Nash grunted and thought how fitting: Those birds are nasty creatures, aggressive and always defending their territory. He had seen those birds pecking at horses if they came too near their turf. Nash shook his head from side to side and thought that he'd better stay clear of Tanya, not get involved when Daniel was still in the picture.

CHAPTER EIGHT

Later that week, Tanya bustled around the house getting ready for Miranda and the baby's homecoming. She cleaned, fluffed pillows and went grocery shopping, stocking the fridge, cupboards, and filled a large bowl with fresh apples, oranges and bananas. Miranda would need a lot of healthy food to provide nutrients for her nursing baby. Tanya heard a car door slam and peeked out the window. As she went to open the door for Miranda, a sudden surge of anger went through her body. It felt weird for her to be welcoming the new family home. Hank should have been the one to escort his new baby into their home. Why did he have to screw things up?

Tanya took in a breath and sighed out her hard feelings. "Welcome home, mama."

Miranda smiled. "I'm so glad to be out of that hospital. I can finally relax with my Emily." She headed toward the porch with a cute bundle wrapped in her arms.

Tanya held the handmade walnut door Hank crafted for them and waited until Miranda and the baby were through. She watched as Ben trotted to greet Miranda, whining and wagging his tail voraciously, his whole black and tan body shaking with excitement.

Miranda bent slightly to pet Ben and let him sniff her bundle. "Hey, buddy. This is your baby sister." Ben licked

Emily's face. Miranda straightened, carrying Emily into the living room.

Tanya went outside to help Justine with Miranda's suitcase, a welcome home package of baby supplies from the hospital, and congratulatory flowers from friends and family.

Once they were all inside, they settled into a terracotta orange leather couch and matching La-Z-Boy, hand-me-downs from Hank's grandmother, and chatted. Tanya started in. "Ran, she is so beautiful. I haven't seen Emily in a couple days, and she looks bigger already."

Miranda smiled as she looked at her sleeping baby. "She gained half a pound in a week." She took off a knitted cap from Emily's head and smoothed her hair. "She's got quite the appetite for sure."

"I bought a whole bunch of food. I read in one of your books that moms need a lot of calories because they burn so much from nursing."

Justine smiled as she looked at Miranda. "When you were little, moms weren't encouraged to nurse their babies. I fed you a bottle from the very first day." She frowned. "I wish things had been different."

Miranda looked at Justine and then at Tanya. "Thanks, you two." She scanned Emily with her glowing eyes. "I don't know what I would have done without your help." She glanced up and her eyes shined with puddles of tears.

Tanya and Justine each took a side and sat next to Miranda. Justine said, "We're here for you, honey."

Ben circled around and curled his body at Miranda's feet.

Tanya nodded. "Whatever you need."

"Right now, I could use a shower and a nap."

Justine said, "I can stay while Emily sleeps. Go ahead, dear, take some time for yourself."

"I'm going out to the barn and see if Nash needs help with anything." Tanya grabbed her jacket out of the closet and slipped on her boots. "Get some rest, Ran."

Justine scooped up the sleeping baby and then Miranda went to the door and gave Tanya a hug. "Thanks, again, Tonny."

She closed the door behind her and then headed for the barn.

CHAPTER NINE

The muddy ground stuck to the bottom of her sloggers and made a sucking sound as Tanya trudged to the barn. The spring breeze had a bite, and she held her jacket close until she passed through the wide-open barn door. She checked the stalls, and they were empty. There was nobody in the barn. Outside, she spotted Nash circling Hank's big Quarter Horse on a lunge rope in the corral.

Even though there was a chill in the spring air, Nash had his shirt off. The lean muscles on his chiseled back glistened in the afternoon sun. Tanya's breath caught in her throat. It took a moment for her to gain composure.

As Tanya approached the corral, she said, "Red's got some spunk today."

"We've been going at it for the last twenty minutes. Seems like he could canter all day."

"With all that's been going on, don't suppose he's been ridden in a while." Tanya stepped on the bottom panel of the fence and leaned on the top wooden plank. "How long you stayin?"

"As long as I can, but my boss needs me to run cattle to higher ground for grazing, since the snow is melting."

Tanya watched as the large sorrel went round the corral, the weight of his hooves thundering, much like the sensation her heart made when she watched Nash exercising Red. There was a lot unsaid between them. That week, she had felt a strong connection but stayed clear of Nash as much as she could. She noticed his breath quickening every time they were near and sensed he felt the same way. The more she tried to ignore her feelings for Nash, the more they grew.

It wouldn't work and she knew it. They were from different worlds. The idea of them getting together was ridiculous and made her doubt her sanity. He was a loner, a guy who wanted to be free in the wild open range, riding horses and without having any restrictions or commitments. Tanya was a free spirit but her whole life was about discipline and super focus and commitment to her team, to her coach, to herself and oh, yes, to Daniel. To Daniel. Why was she even having these thoughts? She muttered under her breath. "Stop it. Right. Now."

"You say something?"

She looked up and there he was. Nash was standing in front of her. He slipped his arms through a shirt that had been flung over the fence, and the blue and black flannel settled over his shoulders as he buttoned the front.

Red came up to the fence. Tanya reached out to pet Red's face. He nickered. Gathering her thoughts and reigning them in, she stroked the soft auburn fur on his nose. "He's a force of nature. Yet he's so gentle." When Red lowered his head onto her shoulder, she scooped up his red forelock and smoothed it down the middle of his head. "He's such a beauty."

"That he is. A gentle giant."

They stood, Nash on one side of the fence and Tanya on the other, their heads only a few inches apart, as they admired Red for a few moments. Tanya could feel Nash's eyes on her. She took a quick glance, and his clear gray eyes looked at her, deep into her soul. She shivered with feelings of closeness she had never felt before with anyone. Even though they had only talked a handful of times since they'd met a few months back, Tanya felt like Nash really knew her.

When she looked at Nash, instead of looking away, he moved toward her, if only an inch. But she felt the heat between them rise to what felt like the tropics. This circle of closeness felt like a moment in time that no one could touch and that they were the only beings in the world. A giant horse stood guard as they shared this space that fostered a deep connection.

Their intimate moment was interrupted by a voice that seemed far in the distance. "Hey, guys."

Instantly, Nash stepped away and Red jerked his big head from Tanya's shoulder. The moment had been aborted. And the chill of the cool spring air filled Tanya's lungs.

They looked up to see Larry, Miranda's cousin, heading towards them carrying a huge sack of feed over his shoulder.

After her shower and before hopping into bed, Miranda peeked out the window. Looking at the horses, even for an instant, always grounded her and made her feel calm. Her eyes went out to the pasture to Mandy first, then Rocko. Her eyes then slid over to the corral, and spotted Tanya and Nash close together with Red. Really close together. What was that all about? She watched them for a couple minutes until she felt like she was intruding on a private moment and let the curtain fall. She got into bed and pulled the thick, fluffy comforter over her to settle in. Birthing a baby was exhausting and she would take advantage of this time to sleep. She'd talk to Tanya later about that moment with Nash and find out the scoop.

CHAPTER TEN

Larry said, "I've got a truck load of grain that Hank ordered a few weeks back. Is he around? I can ask him."

Nash and Tanya glanced at each other. Nash spoke up, "I'll show you where to stack them."

Tanya said, "I'll take care of Red. Go ahead and help Larry." Tanya climbed over the fence and jumped down beside Red. She took hold of the lead rope and started walking Red around the corral to cool him down. She glanced at the maple and walnut trees along the cornfield edges a mile away. What would they tell people about Hank and why he was gone? Or would they just keep it a secret? She'd ask Miranda later and see what the status quo would be.

After Red had cooled down, she led him into the barn. Larry, Nash, and a teenage girl were carrying the bags of feed and stacking them in the back corner of the barn. The girl put her bag in the pile and walked toward them as Tanya was hooking Red up to the grooming station. She hooked one line to his halter, then came around underneath his head to the other side to hook the opposite ring on his halter.

She glanced up and there was the girl petting Red's back. "He's so beautiful." Her big brown eyes bugged. "And big." She was about Tanya's size, petite and reminded Tanya of herself at that age. Curious and in the mix of things.

Tanya smiled. "He's a gentle giant." She bent to get a brush. "What's your name?"

"I'm Stephanie, Larry's daughter."

Tanya started to brush Red's back. She stopped and then turned. "You want to help brush him?"

Stephanie's eyes brightened. "I'd love to."

Tanya handed her a curry comb from the grooming box. "Just go around on his fur in circles. Like this." She demonstrated firmly, but gently circling the round metal comb over the horse's hind quarters. "But don't go on any of his bony areas or his face."

Stephanie took the comb. "I've never groomed a horse before. This is fun."

"You ever ridden?"

"Once, when we went to the fair. You know those ponies that go in a circle?"

"Maybe someday Miranda will teach you how to ride a horse."

Stephanie looked at Tanya and curled her long brown hair behind her ear. "She's my second cousin, ya know."

"That's right. Miranda's dad was *your* dad's brother."

Stephanie kept circling her comb around Red's fur. He seemed to relax and enjoy all the attention.

"You're a natural with animals. I can tell."

"I love dogs and cats. I like horses too, but I've never been around them much." She stopped grooming for a moment and pet Red's face. "I've never told anybody this, but I want to be a vet just like Miranda."

Tanya stood up from picking dirt out of Red's hoof. "You do?" She smirked. "What grade are you in?"

"I'm graduating this spring."

Tanya pondered this information for a few minutes. "How'd you like to have a job helping Miranda?"

Stephanie jumped and squealed. "I'd love that." The movement and high-pitched noise startled Red, and he jerked his head up and backed away from the grooming ties.

"One thing you need to remember when you're around horses. Don't make any sudden movements and use a soft calming voice. They can startle easily. Even Red, here."

Larry called out from the doorway of the barn. "Come on Steph, I'm leaving."

Stephanie handed the comb to Tanya. "I'd better go. Thanks for letting me brush him." She said in a low voice, almost a whisper, "And thanks for the job."

Tanya snickered. "I'll need to ask Miranda if it's ok first."

Stephanie nodded and headed for Larry's truck.

⚡

Once inside the house, Tanya took a shower after the four hours she'd spent grooming and mucking out stalls. She came into the living room. Miranda was nursing Emily. "Where's Justine?"

"I told her to go home, and I'd call her if I needed her. After all, she is only across the yard." She looked at Tanya. "Besides, I have my bestie to help."

"About that." Tanya sat at one end of the couch and hesitated. "I've got to get back to Colorado and back on my training schedule."

Miranda put her hand on her forehead. "I'm sorry, Tonny. I've been so caught up with Emily that I entirely forgot you have a life of your own. I am so grateful for your help."

"I know Ran, I wouldn't miss meeting little Emily."

"When do you have to leave?"

"I should really go in a couple days."

Miranda scrunched her face.

Tanya put her hand up. "I know. I know. It seems like I just got here." She shrugged her shoulders. "My coach has been very patient with my coming and going on these short trips to Iowa."

Miranda lowered her head and looked at Emily who'd fallen asleep.

"I'm just not sure how much more he'll let me get away with." Tanya shifted her body and sat crossed legged on the couch. "I'm nervous he'll give my place away on the Olympic team."

Miranda sat quietly for a few moments. "I know you are in a tricky situation with me and your gymnastics. And I wouldn't ask any other time." She grimaced. "But Hank has put me in a compromising place with our baby and my new practice."

They continued sitting in silence. Tanya wasn't sure what to say. She really had a lot of nasty things to say about Hank. But he was Miranda's husband and the father of Emily. She needed to be careful.

Miranda began to cry. "How could he do this? Why didn't he tell me what was going on? I feel like there is this whole secret life that he kept from me. I just don't know what to do." She sniffed and wiped her nose with the burp cloth she had on her shoulder.

Tanya put her hand on Miranda's knee. "We'll figure it out. Your mom is right next door. I'll help you with a plan to do both, take care of Emily and your vet practice."

Miranda grunted a growl. "I'm so angry I could spit. He made some stupid choices and left me out." She shook her head. "I don't know if we can get back from this."

Emily started to cry. Miranda soothed her and gently put her head on her shoulder and patted her back. "I'm sorry, sweety. I'm getting you upset too. Your daddy is a great big dodo head."

Tanya smirked. "He has screwed up big time, for sure." She smiled as Emily nestled into Miranda. "Have you talked to him at all?"

Miranda shook her head. "I wouldn't know what to say. I don't want to be fake. So, if I said anything at all it would be mean. I know I have to talk to him eventually. I just don't know when."

Tanya felt a little sorry for Hank. His family was miles away from him and he was missing out. His poor choices led him to where he was now, locked up, and far from those he loved.

Miranda got up from the couch and gently laid Emily down in her basinet near the couch. "She's fallen asleep."

"Why don't you relax? I'll make you some food."

"Thanks, Tonny." Miranda went back to the couch and stretched out. "I'm just going to lie down for a few minutes. I didn't get very much sleep last night. Emily was up every two hours to eat." Once she was snuggled in with an afghan she closed her eyes.

A few minutes later Tanya left the kitchen and came out into the living room with a tray of food. She smiled when she realized Miranda was sound asleep. Tanya set the tray down with a ham and cheese sandwich and apple onto the coffee table.

Tanya pivoted and went to the guest room. All the drama of the day had made her tired. She'd get a good night's rest and tackle her conversation about hiring Miranda's cousin, Stephanie, to help Miranda in the clinic, tomorrow. She wouldn't be easily convinced. Miranda could be stubborn and wanted to do everything herself, but she'd have to agree to it if Tanya was going to get back to training for the Olympics.

CHAPTER ELEVEN

In the middle of the night, Tanya woke to a noise that sounded like a cat meowing. It was pitch dark and she thought a few moments as to where she was. That's right. She was at Miranda's house. But what was that noise? She turned on the light on the bedside table and slipped on her robe.

Tanya stepped into the hallway and tiptoed out into the living room and spotted Miranda trying to comfort Emily. "I know you're hungry. Yes, I know." Miranda helped her baby latch on, and Emily began nursing and the crying stopped.

Half awake, Tanya walked a few steps toward Miranda. "Everything ok? Anything I can help with?"

"No. Thanks." She glanced at Tanya. "Welcome to my world. Where sleep is a luxury."

"Ok, then. Night." Tanya gladly walked back to her bed and crawled in. She fell fast asleep.

Later, she was abruptly pulled out of her dreams of backhand springs and beam dismounts. She looked at the digital clock on the dresser across from the bed. Only 2:00 am. She had only slept a couple hours since the last time she'd been woken up by Emily's cry for food. She put a pillow over her ears and tried to drown out the noise.

At 4:30 she woke again. And then again at 6:00. At that time, she got up, slipped her jeans and shirt on. She looked in the mirror as she tied her hair in a ponytail. "I might as well go get some work done in the barn." She pulled some socks on and then went out to the kitchen to make some coffee. Tanya knew one thing; she wasn't going to get any rest staying with Miranda. Babies had their own sleep schedule. Tanya would rather sleep in the barn with the horses and cats than one more night in the house with that noisy baby running the house.

Miranda was on the couch again, nursing Emily. "Morning, friend." Her face was pale and gaunt. "Are you still my friend after waking you up? I hope you didn't hear us after midnight."

Tanya sighed. "I don't know how you do it?" She went over to the coffee maker and put some scoops of coffee into the decanter. "Would a cup of coffee help?"

She twisted her lips. "I'm not supposed to have coffee while I'm nursing. Everything I eat is everything the baby eats. Probably not a good idea to get Emily addicted to coffee." She faked a smile. "At least until she starts school."

Once the coffee had brewed, Tanya poured herself a large mug and sat down in a chair opposite the couch. "Ran, this is probably not a good time, but I need to ask." She took a long draw of the strong coffee she'd brewed. "What are we supposed to tell people about Hank?"

Miranda's eyes bugged and then her lids looked heavy.

"I know it's a weird question, but Larry asked about Hank yesterday. He wanted to know where to put the feed Hank had ordered weeks ago. He asked if Hank was around so he could talk to him. Nash and I avoided the question and kept things moving, but I'd like to know what to tell people in the future if anyone asks."

"I'm not sure yet." A thin line spread across her lips. "I've got enough to handle as it is."

"I know, Ran. Just asking."

"I know this has made things complicated for everyone. Once I get into a routine and get some rest, I'll figure things out."

"That brings me to another question."

Miranda shot a look at Tanya.

"What would you think about hiring your cousin, Stephanie, for a job as your assistant?"

"Absolutely not." Miranda shook her head. "Besides, she's only in high school."

"She's graduating in a couple months. She'd be great."

"How do you know?"

"She helped me groom Red yesterday." Tanya smiled. "I think she'd be a natural with the animals."

Miranda kept quiet.

"Besides she talked about wanting to be a veterinarian. Just like her cuz. She's got it in her blood, Ran."

Miranda rolled her eyes and sighed. "I don't know. I'll think about it."

They sat in the early morning silence for a few minutes.

"I have something to ask you."

Tanya's eyebrows raised. "What could that be?"

Miranda quirked a smile. "What is going on with you and Nash?

Tanya's face felt hot. "What are you talking about?"

"You know exactly what I'm talking about." Miranda flipped her long blond hair over her shoulder and batted her eyes. "You. Nash. Big Red. Out in the corral."

"I was just helping Nash with Hank's horse."

"Hmmmm. Hmmmm."

"Really, Ran. We've been taking care of the horses is all." Tanya sounded like a fraud as she heard the words come out of her mouth. She knew Miranda was right. Miranda was her best friend, and she often knew what was going on with Tanya before Tanya could realize it in herself.

But Tanya still didn't want to believe the feelings she had for Nash. They could be stuffed down when he wasn't around, but as soon as she was in the same room as him, all bets were off. She became a pool of jelly. But she would try harder to get rid of those feelings. And she knew for sure she didn't want to talk to Miranda or anyone else for that matter about Nash. Her place was with Daniel. And that was that.

Tanya swallowed the last bit of coffee in her mug. "What can I do for you the last couple days I'm here?"

Miranda's face sagged. "You really have to go?"

Tanya had never seen Miranda so needy. Her friend was always so strong and self-reliant. If she didn't have the Olympics on the road ahead of her, she'd stay and help out Miranda on the farm and get a job somewhere. But the Olympics was her dream. Even though she felt guilty about leaving and going back to Colorado, she wasn't going to give that up for anything or anyone.

"My mom is coming over later this morning." Miranda cocked her head. "Could you check my messages on the answering machine? Also, could you put a new message on there that says I'll be back in the clinic in a couple days?"

"Are you sure that's not too early? You just had a baby."

"I'll figure it out."

The guilt Tanya felt had gone up the Richter scale a couple notches. But still Tanya had to stay strong. No matter what. She was going to the Olympics.

CHAPTER TWELVE

anya went out to Miranda's office that was attached to the barn. She paused to look at the sign beside the door that read, *Miranda Graaf, DVM* and smiled, proud of her friend. She stepped inside and listened to the answering machine, taking notes about any messages that were left for Miranda. Once she finished, she went through the connecting door to the barn to help with the chores.

She slid the barn door open, and Rocko and Mandy stood, saddled and ready to be ridden. "What...?"

Nash smiled. "I figured the horses could use the exercise and you talked about how you liked riding Rocko." Mandy pawed at the cement, throwing her gray head up and down, impatient to get going.

Well, I guess they do need to be ridden, and this is part of taking care of horses, making sure they get exercise. She giggled. "I'm excited. I've missed riding." She scooted into the tack room and grabbed some riding boots and slipped them on and hurried to Rocko's side. "Let's go."

They rode down the driveway and along the road's shoulder until they crossed the pavement onto a two-track dirt trail. Tanya shifted her weight, hearing the creaking sound of the leather saddle and felt lighter and more carefree than she had in months as they rode through the woods and fields. They saw a couple pheasants in the brush fluttering their brilliant brown and maroon feathers. Tanya ran her fingers through Rocko's auburn mane as they continued forward. "The Rockies are an amazing sight but there is something pretty and comforting about Iowa and its farms and nature."

"I definitely like the mountains, but I know what you mean about the Midwest."

They were gone for about an hour and most of the time rode in silence except for the rhythmic clomp clomp of the horses' hooves on dirt. The morning sun seemed to smile on them and the light breeze swept across her face and arms. Tanya felt relaxed and when they returned to the driveway felt disappointed that the ride was almost over. She noticed a car in the driveway and wondered who was visiting Miranda.

They dismounted and slipped the saddles off the horses, and for the time being, flung the tack over the side of the fence. They began walking the horses inside the corral to cool them down.

Just then, Tanya glanced sideways as Daniel came out of the barn. A flash of heat pricked the skin all over her body. "Daniel. What a surprise."

Daniel had confusion and irritation in his voice and his face looked like he was trying hard to be cool about seeing Tanya riding horses with Nash. His voice sounded flat. "Have a nice ride?"

Tanya thought she'd just go with it. "It was great. Perfect day for a ride." Still leading Rocko, she went up and kissed his cheek. "Want to walk with us?"

Daniel pulled her in and gave her a kiss on the mouth, almost as if claiming his territory. "Sure. I can walk."

Nash said, "Why don't I take the horses and you two can have some time?"

Daniel said, "Thanks, bud. That'd be great."

Tanya looked at Nash and then Daniel and then back again to Nash. "Thank you. I appreciate it. And thanks for the ride. It was fun."

⚡

Nash led the horses around to the opposite side of the corral and out of ear shot, Daniel said, "What are you doing riding with that cowboy?"

"The horses needed exercising. Besides, it was nice to get a ride in before I get back to training."

Daniel took her hand, and they walked to Miranda's house. "That's why I'm here. To bring you back."

She turned to look at him. The late morning sun was glaring in her eyes. She felt warm even though it was a cool morning. "What? You're summoning me back to Colorado?"

"Your coach said he was concerned about you getting back to train."

Tanya was skeptical that her coach actually talked about this to Daniel. In fact, she'd called her coach the night before, and they agreed she could stay another day. "My coach gave me until tomorrow last night when I talked to him."

"I was worried you'd get stuck here somehow." Daniel squeezed her shoulder. "You're a good friend to Miranda. I know you want to help. But you have your life too." He shook his head from side to side. "I think she's taken advantage of you. She needs to understand that. Plus, she's got her mom."

Tanya told herself earlier that day that she wasn't going to let anything get in the way of the Olympics. Plus, she was twenty-five. Gymnasts often retired before they hit mid-twenties. This was her last chance. Another four years, she'd be too old. Maybe she had gotten sidetracked by getting too involved in Miranda's life. Maybe he was right. She scrunched her forehead. "How'd you get here? Did you fly?"

"I drove straight through and just arrived here a few minutes ago."

She looked at the car in the driveway. "That's not your car."

"It's a rental. Maybe there's a flight we could take tonight or first thing."

Tanya felt pulled in several directions. Her coach was giving her the go ahead to help Miranda, and yet she could read between the lines. If she didn't get back to training soon, he was going to drop her from the Olympic team. She needed to get more serious about gymnastics.

Still, guilt about not staying longer to help Miranda since Hank wasn't there, weighed heavily on her. Miranda was her best friend after all. Tanya could see it in Miranda's wide eyes, searching for answers and struggling to comprehend her life. She needed her help. Miranda was going through one of the toughest times in her life.

And now Daniel was pulling her along, wanting more from her too. They were in a relationship, but they were also partners in their dream to be Olympic athletes, striving for that gold. She'd never had anybody in her life who understood what that meant like Daniel had.

And then there was Nash. The fondness she felt was real. Her heartbeat doubled as she thought about him. Maybe the feelings were a scapegoat, allowing her to go to a place in her mind that was exciting and fun and pleasurable, away from her strict training regime. Tingles of tiny fireworks scattered throughout her body and slid down her spine, as she glanced at Nash leading Rocko and Red around the corral, their sweaty backs glistening from their ride earlier.

Nash didn't demand anything from her. He just allowed her to be. To be wherever she was in her life at that moment. He didn't put any pressure on her or ask anything from her. He just let her feel whatever she needed to feel. Just like that moment when she felt lost and cried and they sat on the bench in the barn. He was just there for her, allowing her to be. With the memory of that moment her lungs expanded, allowing her to take in a deep breath.

Tanya turned to look at Daniel and she felt more confused than ever. What was she going to do? "This is all too much. Just give me a moment. I'm going to talk to Miranda. You wait here."

He scowled. "But…"

Tanya put her hand up. "Just. Wait." She walked toward the door of Miranda's house. Tanya didn't know what she'd say to her friend. But she had to start somewhere with all the guilt, frustration, and confusion that were somersaulting inside her belly. She'd figure out what to do once she and Miranda talked. After all, she and Miranda went way back when they were kids, stretched out on their bareback horses as they munched on grass and the two girls talking about boys, school and their parents. Miranda had always been her rock. Together, they would come up with a plan.

But now things were different. The last few months Miranda needed help from others more than ever. She had a baby to take care of and a veterinarian practice to run. By herself.

Tanya clasped the door handle, took a deep breath and stepped inside the house. Miranda was crying, the baby was crying. Justine was trying to help give Emily a bath in the kitchen sink. Babies were so slippery. It was like trying to take hold of a fish swimming in a pond. Tanya approached the kitchen. "Is there anything I can do to help? Get a towel?" She grimaced. "Get you an aspirin?"

Justine let out a chuckle. "This is Emily's first bath. It's always a trick trying to get a handle on this bathing thing."

Tanya patted Miranda on the arm. "Hang in there, Ran. You're doing great." Feeling helpless, and way out of her element, she said, "I'm just going to be in the bedroom changing." Tanya headed for the guest room. She sat down on the bed and thought about what to do. Next thing she knew she was packing all her stuff. It was time to go back to Colorado. Time to get serious about training for the Olympics. Miranda had Justine and Richard to help her. She didn't know how long Nash was going to stay but they could always hire some help. It wasn't her responsibility to put her life on hold and step in as a permanent fixture. Miranda and Hank needed to figure out their life on their own.

Ben lumbered into her room and sat next to her feet.

Tanya chuckled. "Too much for you?" She stroked the dog's black and tan ears and head. "You're a good boy, aren't you?"

Tanya went out into the kitchen, her suitcase rolling behind her. She hugged Miranda. "Ran, I've got to go. You have enough help. It's time I get back to training. Soon I'll be traveling with the team to Denver, Salt Lake City, and then Phoenix for competition.

Miranda brushed tears from her eyes. "Sorry, I'm hormonal."

"You've got a lot going on." She bent to give Emily a kiss on the cheek. "You take care of your momma, little one." She looked at Miranda. "You'll figure everything out."

"We're counting on you getting a gold medal in September." Justine gave Tanya a hug. She smiled. "We'll be alright."

When Tanya reached the door, she turned, saying, "I'm only a phone call away."

Miranda said, "Call me when you get in."

And Tanya left, closing the door behind her. Outside, she said to Daniel, "Take my things. I'll be right back."

He took her coat and suitcase. When she headed for the barn, he folded his arms and cocked his head.

Tanya went into the barn, looking for Nash. She overheard him on the phone. "I'll let Miranda know when your hearing is." He moved his head from side to side. "I can't promise you she'll come to it."

Tanya came up beside him. "Tell him he's a jerk and to hurry back and be a dad. Miranda needs him."

Nash said into the receiver, "Hear that?" He nodded. "Yep. Ok. Bye."

When he got off the phone Tanya said, "I'm going back to Colorado. I wanted to say goodbye before I left."

The look in Nash's eyes sent a warmth throughout Tanya's heart. She had an instant longing to surrender into his arms, melting into his hug. But she knew that she had to be strong and keep moving. "Thanks for all your help. Hank is lucky to have you as his friend."

Nash gave her a long look before he spoke. "Miranda is just as lucky to have you." He tipped his head downward and adjusted his black Stetson. "You'll be back soon?"

"I wish. But I'll be deep into training at camp getting ready for this fall."

He smiled. "Good luck. I know you'll do good." He reached out and lightly touched her hand. "Bring us back a medal."

The pull to stay was so strong that it felt like being on the balance beam doing the splits, one leg going one direction, the other going the opposite but she turned and walked briskly out of the barn. She opened the front passenger door and settled into Daniel's car. "Let's get back." Tanya looked in the side mirror and saw Nash glance at their car as he led Penny and her foal that Hank had bought a month prior, outside heading for the pasture.

Daniel sped towards I-80, west, towards Colorado. Tanya rested her head on the headrest and closed her eyes, getting ready for the long drive back to her world of balance beams and backflips. She'd need the rest.

CHAPTER THIRTEEN

The following week Hank was taken by a police officer to the courthouse for his sentencing: Hank's steps choppy from the ankle shackles. He met with his attorney and then waited in a locked room with other inmates. After several minutes, a different officer came to get him, and they stepped inside the courtroom. Hank smelled the polished wood; so much wood: the judge's bench and witness stand, the wooden railings separating the proceedings from the gallery benches. Off to the side even, the jury box was made of mahogany. Cruisers sounded their sirens as they passed by outside. Large fans whooshed on the ceiling. A court reporter sat at her desk, hands in her lap waiting for the hearings to begin.

Spectators filled the room. Hank presumed family members and friends of inmates. He hoped that Miranda would be there too, but his heart plummeted when he scanned the room and didn't see her.

He had opted for a court-appointed attorney as he didn't want to spend money on a big-wig attorney. Hank knew he was taking a risk, and the judge could give him anything. He hoped he'd be released on house arrest so that he could at least be with Miranda and get to know his new baby. Hank and his attorney settled in at the table reserved for the defendant. At the table across the aisle was the prosecutor. He gave Hank a stern look when Hank looked his way. The cuffs on Hank's wrists felt tight and were pinching his skin. He fidgeted and tried to get comfortable. He felt hot in his orange jumpsuit.

The court clerk entered the courtroom from a doorway at the front. She stood in front of the crowded room and said, "All rise. Judge T. J. Thomas presiding." Everyone stood. A tall man in his fifties walked toward the bench in the front of the court room.

Hank's mouth felt dry. He took one last glance back to see if Miranda had come, and he spotted her in the back row of the courtroom. His heart leapt into his throat. She looked more beautiful than he'd remembered when he saw her two weeks before when she glowed with pregnancy. Her long blond hair glistened in the overhead lights in the courtroom. Yet she looked pale, and her eyebrows scrunched together in worry. Hank caught her eye and smiled. His eyes fell to the bundle in her arms. Emily! His eyes filled as he longed to hold his brand-new daughter. His heart ached. Miranda had refused to take any of his calls for the last two weeks, and he was shocked that she was there. His gut wrenched at the thought of putting her through all this. Why hadn't he taken care of his past before he married Miranda? He was such an idiot. He didn't deserve her.

She flashed a slight smile, her chin rigid as if holding back emotions.

Next to Miranda, Justine held herself erect, a stern pinched look on her face. Hank's eyes traveled across the aisle to the other side of the courtroom. A tall, wiry cowboy, a man in his sixties, rose in the last row. He swiped his weathered hand over his tan face and then placed his dark grey Stetson at his side. What was Walt, his old boss from Wyoming doing there? Hank hadn't seen Walt since he'd left Wyoming over two years before.

Judge Thomas took his seat, adjusted the sleeve on his black robe and pounded a gavel. "Please be seated."

Hank's attorney nudged him to sit down.

The wooden benches creaked as people sat and shifted, settling before the hearing began. The shuffling of papers as the judge and attorneys prepared for the hearing made Hank more nervous than he had been when he came in.

With a gravelly voice, the judge rattled off some facts. He lowered his eyes to read the file, and his bald head gleamed from the reflection of the fluorescent lights on the ceiling.

When he finished, he placed his reading glasses beside him. "I understand that we're here because a Mr. Hank Driskill was charged two years ago in Laramie County in the city of Cheyenne with assault. Mr. Driskill failed to fulfill his probation and did not get approval from the courts to leave this county. Apparently, Mr. Driskill has been living in Dewitt, Iowa for the past two years. He has spent two weeks in jail and is now here for sentencing." He looked up from the papers in front of him. "Mr. Driskill, do you care to say anything before we proceed?"

Hank's attorney leaned over. "Stand up Hank. Tell him how you feel."

The fact that Hank had his family and a friend in the court room supporting him hopefully would make a difference to the judge. His attorney had told him that judges liked it when inmates had people showing interest from the outside. It meant the chances were higher that they'd succeed when released from jail.

Hank wished he had a mint or cough drop. He licked his lips hoping to add some lubrication so his teeth wouldn't catch on his lips while he spoke. His heart felt like it was going to leap out of his tight chest. Hank stood and looked at the judge. How could he convey to him and to the people in the room his remorse for being so stupid? And especially, now that he saw Miranda, he wanted her to know that he didn't take this error in judgement lightly. He wished he had told her the moment he received notice in the mail from the plaintiff's attorney about the bar fight and getting arrested when he lived in Wyoming two years prior. But instead, he was all alone in this and everyone else was kept separate from his life.

"Your honor." Hank's voice shook and he cleared his throat. In a stronger tone he said, "I just want you to know that I take full responsibility for my error in judgement. I should have paid attention to the terms of my sentence two years ago when I was here in the court room. I paid my fines and just wanted to get out of town and return home to Iowa where my grandma lived and start anew. I didn't realize at the time that I should have stayed in Cheyenne and fulfilled my probation." He felt the hard stare of everyone in the courtroom and it felt like the air in the room spiked in heat and humidity. "I should have asked an official in the court system if I was free to leave the state. But I didn't and I'm sorry for that." Since he hadn't talked to Miranda about all this, he wanted her to know in a roundabout way that he was truly remorseful and wanted to make it right. His eyes stung. "I have a two-week-old daughter that I haven't met yet and my wife is alone with the responsibilities of caring for our baby and our farm and would like to get home as soon as possible." He heard a low murmur amongst the audience behind him.

With a solemn face the judge folded his arms in front of him as he listened to Hank's story. When Hank finished, the judge said, "I sympathize with your predicament, Mr. Driskill." He looked at his file and then again at Hank. "If your home was in Cheyenne, we could give you home arrest but since you live out of state, you'll need to stay here to fulfill the terms of your sentence. You are sentenced to three months in jail, with work release for community service and one year's probation. The terms of where you will serve your probation upon finishing community service and jail will be determined, depending on your behavior the next three months."

Hank felt like he had been socked in the stomach. He lowered his eyes as the judge stated the terms, realizing he was going to be away from his family for *three* more months: sharing living quarters with men he couldn't trust, always on alert and watching his back, eating tasteless food, confrontations with inmates and guards. But mostly having his freedom taken away made him feel like a caged animal. He didn't know how he was going to get through it. The last two weeks had been hell.

The judge looked at Hank, studying him for a moment. "Are there any questions, Mr. Driskill?"

Hank slowly shook his head from side to side.

"Your future is determined by how you act in jail and in your community service work. The bottom line is that if you stay out of trouble, it will serve you well. Good luck, Mr. Driskill."

His attorney looked at Hank and then said, "If you need anything, let me know." He packed his briefcase with Hank's file then turned and left the courtroom.

A policeman stood beside Hank and said, "Let's go Driskill." They walked toward the side door. Before Hank left the courtroom he glanced to the back where Miranda sat with tears falling down her cheeks. Hank's gut felt like it had been punched with a sledgehammer.

CHAPTER FOURTEEN

Miranda sat there, stunned. Hank wasn't coming home for three months. Three. Whole. Months. Emily would be rolling over, playing with rattle toys, laughing and babbling. She wouldn't recognize Hank's voice. She wouldn't even know him.

Justine leaned in against Miranda and wrapped her arm around her shoulders. "It'll all work out, honey." After a few minutes she whispered, "I'm going to the rest room." She scooted past Miranda and left the court room. On her way out, she bumped into Walt as they both passed through the door to the hallway.

"Excuse me, Ma'am." Walt tipped his cowboy hat as Justine glanced up at the tall, lean cowboy that stood only inches away from her. She smiled slightly and then headed toward the bathroom.

Miranda felt heavy in the seat, like a boulder planted in the ground. She had to put a hand on the wooden bench to hold herself up. Their life was falling apart, falling down a hill and she couldn't stop it. She watched as another inmate was hauled into the courtroom by an officer.

She felt a tap on her shoulder. "Miranda?"

Miranda looked up and Richard was standing in the aisle. They had driven to Wyoming from Iowa the day before and stayed at a hotel so they could make it for Hank's hearing.

They drove all day, stopping only to eat and stretch their legs. "Where's Justine?"

Miranda told herself to move her legs. She clutched the back of the seat in front of her with one hand and the other holding tight to Emily, pulling her lead body upright. She mumbled, "She's in the bathroom."

Richard moved aside as Miranda headed to the door of the courtroom. Her gut gurgled and she felt a hot flash of heat run through her body as she trotted to the ladies' room just as Justine was coming out. She handed Emily to Justine. "Hold her!" Miranda rushed to a stall, shoved the door open and vomited in the toilet. When she finished, she sat on the stool, head in her hands and rocked back and forth. She felt more alone than she'd ever felt before and her whole body hurt with an ache so deep she didn't know if she could make it through the next few months. After several minutes she left the stall, went to the sink and splashed cold water on her face. As she dried her face with a paper towel she looked up to the ceiling. "Help me, Daddy. Help me get through this." She hugged her belly and stood looking in the mirror, taking slow deep breaths, feeling calmer within minutes.

Miranda left the bathroom thinking she'd survive this somehow. Even though her dad had been gone for over two years, she felt Stanley's presence. She'd find a way to plow through the next three months as the family had always done.

Justine gently handed Emily, red faced and crying over to Miranda. They headed for the car and settled in the back seat. Once Miranda began nursing Emily, she stopped crying and eventually drifted off to sleep. Miranda retrieved a cloth diaper from Emily's bag and flopped it over her shoulder. She held her baby to her chest and softly patted her back.

Justine scooted beside Miranda on the back seat and tilted her head examining Miranda. "Ready to get some dinner?"

Miranda felt like she was on autopilot. Her mouth talked to her mom, but she remained separate from her body. "The hearing was rough." She smoothed Emily's hair, looking straight ahead. "It's going to be a long three months."

Miranda noticed her mom shooting a look to Richard sitting in the driver's seat and then back at her. "What are you going to do?"

"What do you mean what am I going to do? He's the one who got us in this mess," Miranda said with a snarl, focusing on her baby. "He's going to miss the first part of her life. Emily won't know her daddy."

Justine patted her daughter's leg. "It'll all work out, you'll see."

Miranda glanced at Justine. She didn't see how. Their marriage had been nothing but secrets and stress. How did they get to this place? They'd only been married a year. And it was one of the worst and the best years of her life all in one.

Once Miranda finished burping Emily, she buckled her into the infant seat. Justine moved to the front seat and then Richard steered his Cadillac onto the road, and they drove through the town of Cheyenne. Emily slept in her car seat and Miranda took note of the saloons, western wear shops, and eateries serving beef, bison, and elk steaks, chops, and ribs. She sighed, taking a mental break from the stressful day at court. Shoppers donned in cowboy hats and boots walked the streets. This was cowboy country. She imagined herself and Hank strolling through the city, hand in hand enjoying the relaxed atmosphere, enjoying a day together. A single tear rolled slowly down her cheek and Miranda leaned her forehead into the glass. It could only go upward from this moment. She'd find a way to plow through the summer until Hank returned.

Justine pointed and said, "Look! That'd be fun to go to," as they passed a giant billboard on the edge of town that sported, *Cheyenne Frontier Days, World's Largest Outdoor Rodeo and*

Western Festival, July 18-27. Cowboys riding bucking broncos and women in western attire navigating horses around barrels donned the large sign.

"Burgers, ok?" Justine nodded and Richard parked his car.

Miranda wasn't hungry but she knew she needed to eat for Emily's benefit.

CHAPTER FIFTEEN

*L*ater that evening, at the jail, Miranda sat in a booth, a phone secured on the wall off to the side. Emily squirmed in a swaddled blanket in Miranda's lap, and she tried her best to keep Emily comfortable by patting her back and talking to her in a soothing voice. It seemed nothing she did helped, and Miranda wondered if her tiny baby could sense Miranda's restlessness as they waited for Hank to appear on the other side of the plexiglass that separated them from an adjoining cubicle.

After several minutes, Hank arrived wearing the same orange jumpsuit he wore in the courtroom. The orange screamed criminal, and the reality of the situation hit Miranda even harder than seeing him earlier that day.

Hank stationed himself at the window and flattened his hand on the plexiglass on his side of the booth. He gazed at Emily, tears streaming down his face and slowly picked up the phone receiver. He motioned for Miranda to pick up her phone.

She grasped the receiver on her side while wrapping her arm around Emily.

"Hi, babe. She's beautiful." A high wind of feelings hit his gut like the eye of a tornado tearing through town.

Miranda felt a mishmash of anger, sadness, and disbelief. The situation felt surreal and out of context for how she and

Hank had once lived. She wanted to yell at him. She wanted to hold him. She wanted to sooth the lines on his tortured face. She missed him. She was so close and yet they were kept apart. What could she say?

"I miss you, babe." He bent his head downward. He swiped his runny nose with the back of his hand and when he looked up again, tears pooled in his eyes. "I am so sorry. I've been an idiot and put you through so much. I am sorry."

She couldn't speak. She just cried. The tears poured out of her eyes like an open faucet spigot.

"Babe. I'm sorry." They both sat and cried, a plexiglass dam separating their pools of pain. Comforting each other would have to wait.

After a few minutes a jail officer came and opened the door on Hank's side. "Driskill, you've got one more minute." Then he stood outside the booth, waiting.

Hank wiped his eyes. "There's so much I want to talk about." He sniffled. "You did good. Emily is amazing. So tiny. I want to be with you both so bad."

The officer came in. "Time to go." Before Hank stood, he put a hand on the glass again. "Please forgive me, Miranda. I love you."

And then he left.

Justine watched as Miranda treaded over to the car, cradling Emily in her arms. Justine had never seen her daughter look like she had at that moment. Anger, sadness, defeat and hurt all wrapped in a package that clouded her face, covering it like a storm rolling across acres of corn fields. Like a tornado warning on the local Davenport news.

When Miranda opened the door, Justine asked, even though she knew it hadn't gone well, "How'd it go, sweetie?"

As Miranda described her visit, Justine felt her insides constrict like wringing out a dish rag. Her only daughter was in pain.

"It's hard seeing him in jail. I can't touch him, and we only have fifteen minutes to talk. Visitation is only twice a week. I don't know how he'll last in there."

Even though Justine wanted to take away the pain like only a mother would, she knew this was something she couldn't do anything about. If she could go inside that jail and demand that her son-in-law, father of her grandchild, be released, throw a fit and yell at the officers and workers inside the jail, she would. But she might end up getting thrown in jail for disturbing the peace. Or she could act like in the old west, breaking in and releasing Hank, tying up the attendants and locking them in a cell.

But this time Justine couldn't take away the pain, she could only be there for Miranda when she needed to talk and let her know that Justine loved her and everything would be ok. Even if Justine wasn't sure herself.

That is what mothers do. Love their children through everything. Oftentimes, it was their journey to walk in life. And as a mother, there was nothing she could do but love them. Miranda and Emily and even Hank.

"He's strong. I'm sure it won't be a picnic." Justine said to Miranda, "But he'll come out ok."

Miranda kissed Emily on her cheek. "I could tell it was torture not holding her." She laid Emily in her car seat and buckled her in.

Richard interjected. "He's paying the price now for his thoughtless actions then. It was bound to catch up to him."

Miranda glared at him. "We all make mistakes. No one is perfect."

"But this was a big one…

Justine squeezed Richard's shoulder, cutting off his words. "Let's go, Richard." She turned back to look at Miranda. "We thought we'd get a head start toward home and drive through the night." She gestured toward the front seat. "Richard had a nap and is raring to go."

Richard pulled his Cadillac out of the parking lot.

Once they were on the I-80 freeway headed east, Miranda fell asleep quickly, and the group started their eleven-hour journey home.

CHAPTER SIXTEEN

They'd traveled two hours down the freeway and the baby started crying. Miranda had slept the entire time. She was as exhausted from the mental stress of Hank being in jail as she was taking care of Emily as a single parent. Because that's what she was. A single parent. She was still married, yes, but she was living as if she was single, taking care of her baby.

Justine tapped Richard on his arm. "Honey, could we take a break? Miranda needs to feed the baby, and I could use a bathroom."

Richard heaved a sigh. "Yeah, I guess. At this rate, we'll make it home in two days."

Justine rolled her eyes. "Really, Richard? This is going to upset your travel plans?" Once he pulled onto an exit ramp, she pointed to McDonalds. "Pull in there. We can go to the bathroom and get something to go. That way it'll make everybody happy." She threw him a look. "And we won't be long."

Miranda lifted Emily out of her car seat and began nursing her. She looked at Justine and then at Richard. "You guys go ahead and use the bathroom."

Richard sighed audibly and opened the door. He slammed it behind him. Miranda jerked in her seat and the baby started crying again. A few feet away from the car, Justine said to Richard, "Why are you being so difficult?"

"I can't believe we came all this way for that loser in jail."

Justine glanced over at the car. "Keep your voice down. Don't talk about Hank that way. He's made a big mistake, yes, but he is still Miranda's husband. And the father of her baby." She scoffed. "You're the one that suggested this trip."

Richard folded his arms in front of him as he leaned on a lightpost near the car. "I'm just tired and want to get home."

She shook her head from side to side. "I'm going inside. You want anything? A burger. Coffee?"

He lifted himself off the pole. "I'll come with you." They walked toward the entrance.

Miranda rolled her eyes. She continued feeding her baby and looked at Emily's angelic face. "I don't like Richard. I don't think he's good for Grandma." She stroked her cheek. "No, he's not, but don't tell Grandma I said that." She gently wiped Emily's face with a washcloth. Miranda picked Emily up from her lap laying her on the seat to change her diaper. "Your daddy is in a tricky situation, but he'll get to be with us again and we can all be a family, for once. You'll see."

Justine and Richard headed toward the car carrying two bags and some beverages. The smell of coffee and French fries filled the car when they opened the doors. Justine handed Miranda a burger and ice water. They finished their break and were on the road again continuing east on I-80, toward home.

The group of weary travelers arrived home the following morning after driving through the night, taking occasional stops for food and gas. Miranda got out of the car, stretched her arms high in the air and glanced over at the sun rising on the horizon of the cornfields. She sighed, glad to finally be home.

She reached in to retrieve Emily who was fast asleep in her car seat.

Justine called out from the opposite side of the Cadillac. "You go on in with the baby, honey. Richard and I will bring your stuff into the house."

"Thanks, Mom. I'm going to put Emily in her crib." Miranda carried Emily, still inside her car seat, to the house. She unlocked the door and went inside. After Miranda put the baby to bed, she went to the kitchen and started the coffee maker. While the aroma of hot coffee, albeit decaffeinated, filled the kitchen, Miranda rested in a chair at the table, folded her arms and thought about their trip. It had been a shock to see Hank behind bars. It was weird talking to her husband through a phone in the wall, separated by glass. Miranda didn't know how their marriage would survive being apart from each other. It seemed like it had been one hardship after another since they married only a year ago. She felt sadness, confusion, and anger because of what Hank had done. But mostly she felt heartache. How could he hurt her by keeping the legal difficulties he was having? From her?

Miranda poured coffee into a *Best Mom in the World* mug Hank had given her for Christmas. They had laughed about how they'd given each other the same mug, only his mug said, *Best Dad in the World*. But she wondered- he certainly hadn't started out the first two weeks as the best dad. She thought about taking a marker and crossing off the *best* on his mug and writing *worst* above it.

Miranda sipped her coffee while she stood at the window looking out their backyard at the sun rising in a deep scarlet striped with jade green that glowed in the sky giving off an eerie warning of trouble ahead. A slight chill ran through her and she forced her mind to focus on what she could do and stop obsessing about what couldn't be helped.

Just then, her mom and Richard came through the door with her suitcase and a couple of bags of Emily's things. Justine said, "This is everything. Do you want me to help you with anything? Watch Emily while you take a shower?"

Richard cleared his throat and gave Justine a stern look.

She glared at him. And then went into the kitchen. She poured herself a cup of coffee. "You're free to go."

He plunked the suitcase and bag he'd been carrying onto the floor. With a firm voice, he said, "I'm going into town to pick up some groceries. Need anything at Hy-Vee?"

"Thank you, Richard. I think we're all set."

Miranda thought for a moment. She could use some milk, and she'd used the last of bread for sandwiches before they left. But before she could say anything Richard left. Her face scrunched. "What is going on with you two?" She gestured. "You've been at each other since we left Cheyenne."

"He's jealous."

"Jealous of what?" Miranda wondered if there was someone else in her mom's life and she'd been so busy she hadn't noticed.

Justine hesitated. "You and the baby."

Her mouth popped open. "What? How could he be jealous of a little baby?"

"Because it takes time away from *him*."

Miranda pressed her hand to Justine's forearm. "Mom. The last thing I want to do is cause friction between the two of you." She set her mug on the table. "Go. Go with him to the store. I'll be fine. I have a baby monitor for when I take a shower. I need to get used to doing things on my own."

Justine's lips pressed together. "He needs to grow up. You go take a shower. I'll check on Emily."

Miranda tipped her head. "Are you sure?"

"Go. Go on."

Miranda kissed her mom on the cheek before heading for the bathroom.

CHAPTER SEVENTEEN

After Miranda took a shower, Justine left and went back to her own house. Miranda put Emily in a stroller and went out to the barn to check on the horses in their stalls. She slid the barn door open and breathed in sweet-smelling timothy hay and the earthy, musky scent of horses as they munched on grain. Miranda smiled and her muscles relaxed for the first time since hearing of Hank's predicament. *This was home* away *from home.* Where she felt at ease having been around horses and animals her whole life.

Miranda scooped Emily and held her against her chest marveling at her baby's sweet face and soft breathing as she slept. Miranda stepped into the tack room looking for some brushes. Nash had left a note on one of the saddles saying he'd left that morning and headed back to his ranching job in Wyoming. Miranda's cousin, Larry, had been kind enough to help Nash take care of the animals while they were away, visiting Hank. She had confided in Larry about Hank's legal issues. He was shocked but eager to help Miranda any way he could.

They had five horses now. Mandy, Rocko, Red, Penny and her filly, Belle. Miranda popped her head into the opening of Penny's stall and smiled. The chestnut mare gathered pellets of grain with her lips and crunched on the golden nuggets, while at the same time Belle nursed, standing beside her mother.

Miranda kept walking and when she reached Mandy's stall she gasped. The horse's gray head hung low, and she didn't respond to Miranda's greeting. Typically, Mandy would nicker and nod her head up and down showing her excitement in seeing Miranda. Miranda placed Emily, still sleeping, in the stroller and then opened the stall and stepped inside. She bent to palpate Mandy's side and belly. Something was wrong with her horse. She had never seen the mare this way before. When Miranda hooked her arm underneath Mandy's head and pulled her gently upward, the horse looked at Miranda with dull eyes. Her bottom lip drooped, and drool trickled onto Miranda's hand.

Miranda strolled Emily in front of her, hurrying past Rocko and Red's stalls and to the side door where she reached in her pocket for keys, fumbling through the collection until she found the right one. Her breathing accelerated as she shoved the key in the keyhole and unlocked the door to her clinic. Emily began to wriggle, and her face squished. Miranda said, "Hang in there, baby. I'll only be a moment." She scurried into the office and grabbed her veterinary bag. Emily started to cry. Miranda raced to Emily and picked her up, holding her against her chest and patting her back. Within minutes Emily calmed down and went back to sleep. Miranda gently placed Emily back in the stroller, covering her with a blanket and pushing the carriage to the outside of Mandy's stall.

Her mind whirled with thoughts of what could be wrong with Mandy. It was certainly different when your own pet was ill. Let alone taking care of a newborn at the same time. It was hard to think straight. Typically, when Miranda treated animals, she went into doctor mode. But Mandy had been with her since she was a teenager, and Miranda had been through a lot. When Miranda's dad was ill, she wept, leaning her head on Mandy many times out in the barn. Mandy had been a source of comfort during her adolescent years and beyond.

A plunk of weight in Miranda's gut told her that Mandy was seriously ill.

Miranda moved her stethoscope along Mandy's chest listening to her heartbeat and lungs. She then pressed the chest piece to the horse's abdomen checking for gut sounds. Next, she scanned the inside of her mouth for any obstruction. Miranda examined her feet, legs and hooves. Everything appeared normal.

Just then, Emily began to whimper, accelerating to a high-pitched wail. Miranda patted Mandy's back, saying, "We'll figure this out, girl."

And then Miranda hurried to Emily's side and picked up a pacifier in a pocket near the back of the stroller. She mumbled, "The nurse told me to wait a couple weeks until you've been nursing a while, but here goes anyway," She gently put the binkie in Emily's mouth, and her baby immediately began sucking.

She quickly took out a syringe from the vet bag and drew some blood from Mandy's neck to be tested in her lab. She drew enough blood so that she could send it away to an outside source for diseases that Miranda couldn't test in her own office.

Emily began to wail again. "I know. It's time to feed you, sweet one."

Miranda deposited the filled vials in her vet bag and jostled the stroller with one hand and the other hand onto Emily, crying. A wave of prickly heat ran through Miranda. Once they made it to her office, she dropped the vet bag on her desk and then sat in a chair, snuggling Emily to her chest. While Emily nursed, she gazed at the precious life dependent on her to stay alive and Miranda thought about how difficult it was going to be continuing her vet practice while taking care of her baby. When Emilly finished nursing Miranda changed her diaper and tucked her into the stroller. She fell asleep once again.

After conducting basic tests such as a complete blood count and a chemistry panel using the centrifuge to separate Mandy's blood and looking at smears under the microscope Miranda found them all normal. She called Federal Express and requested they pick up the remaining blood samples to be overnighted to the Iowa State's veterinarian lab. She called the lab and talked to the supervisor, asking for priority testing. Miranda wanted to get to the bottom of this so she could help Mandy. But for now, she felt helpless and didn't know what else to do except try to make Mandy comfortable.

Leaving Emily asleep in her stroller right inside the entrance to the clinic, Miranda went out into the barn. She crossed her forearms and leaned on the ledge of the door to Mandy's stall, staring at her horse, as if the longer she contemplated the more likely the answer would reach out and pop her in the face. What could it be? She went through different diseases like a file in her mind: Lyme Disease? Mandy was lethargic and her general behavior was different. She didn't seem like the Mandy that Miranda had always known. Could she have Equine Encephalitis or Equine Herpes Virus? Sometimes it could be difficult to diagnose problems with horses. Miranda knew that. But her life had been a whirlwind lately and she didn't trust herself in diagnosing Mandy.

Miranda had just started her own practice eight months prior after she returned from her internship in England and had felt confident about treating patients. Until now. She needed some help. Back in her office, she leafed through the index file on her desk and landed on the name Gerrit De Van, veterinarian. Doc Tanner, her mentor since childhood, had recommended him, and had consulted with him on his equine expertise a few times before Tanner retired.

Miranda had asked Tanya to call Dr. De Van when Miranda was in the hospital. He had a practice in Clinton, Iowa, one town over. Miranda had talked to him on the phone when she was on bed rest a couple months before asking him to cover for her for after she had her baby. He remembered Miranda from a lecture he had given in one of her classes at Iowa State in Ames, Iowa about various treatments for horses. He had said he was more than happy to fill in for Miranda until she returned to work.

She respected how deeply Dr. De Van cared for animals, hearing about him from other practitioners. Miranda dialed his number.

An hour later, after making Mandy as comfortable as possible, trying to get her to eat and drink water without success, Miranda waited for Dr. De Van in front of the barn as she held Emily who was swaddled and fast asleep against her chest. She appreciated him making a special farm visit, traveling twenty miles in the middle of his day to see Mandy. Miranda had offered to trailer Mandy to his farm, but Dr. De Van insisted that he come to her and check things out. When he arrived, he parked in front of the barn and got out of his black dually truck. She waved.

Miranda took note of Dr. De Van as he walked toward her. He reminded her of a Viking warrior with his tall and robust stature, broad shoulders, blond hair, and light blue eyes.

She flashed a quick smile. "Thank you for coming so quickly, Dr. De Van."

He stretched his arm outward, and they shook hands. "Please, call me, Gerrit."

"I'll show you to Mandy's stall." Miranda led Gerrit into the barn and to the ailing horse's stall. Mandy hung her head and struggled to winny.

"I've conducted every blood test I could think of: CBC and chemistry panel. And sent away samples by Fed Ex to Iowa State."

Gerrit crossed the stall to Mandy's side, and she backed up a couple steps. He stroked her neck and back as he said, "Easy girl." Mandy settled and then Gerrit palpated her abdomen and listened to her heart, lungs, and gut with his stethoscope. Miranda observed his calm and soothing nature. Despite his size, Gerrit was gentle and agile as he stepped around the dappled horse and ran his large hands along her legs and feet. His clear blue eyes were razor focused as he looked inside Mandy's mouth and then shined a light in her eyes, looking for injury or infection. Time stood still as he masterfully checked her out like an artist examining a painting.

Gerrit removed the stethoscope ear pieces, curving them around his shoulders, looking at Miranda. "I think it's enterolithiasis."

Her eyes bugged. "She hasn't shown any signs of colic or intestinal discomfort." Shaking her head, she said, "I know Arabians have more enteroliths than other breeds, but she's never had a problem before. Besides, horses in hot, dry climates mostly have intestinal objects that won't pass. I've always been careful what she eats." She ran her hand over Mandy's withers. "What makes you think it's that? You haven't taken an x-ray."

"I had a patient a couple months ago from Arizona traveling through on their way to Michigan. They were taking their horse to a horse show, and he was sluggish and seemed depressed, so they brought him in. Same symptoms as Mandy: lowered head, apathy, didn't seem in discomfort, just no energy. I could take an x-ray at my clinic if you'd like." The empathy in his eyes softened to a lake blue. "I know it's hard to see clearly when it's your own. I lost my horse I'd had since I was a kid a few years back. It was hard." He reached outward to place his hand on her arm. "It could be she has a rock, twine or sand stuck and blocking her colon. We'll figure it out. Two heads and all."

Emily began fidgeting on Miranda's chest. "My daughter's hungry. I'll trailer Mandy over after I feed her."

"If you'll let me, I can hitch your trailer onto my truck and take Mandy back with me."

She exhaled. It was weird having this kind man helping her. Hank would have been the one assisting her with this. He would have trailered Mandy to Dr. De Van's office, especially with a new baby to care for. Emily started to fuss and then cried. Gerrit glanced at Emily.

Miranda gestured toward the barn door. "The trailer is outside at the side of the barn. You need help hooking it up?"

Gerrit nodded toward Emily. "You take care of your little one. I got this."

Miranda hurried toward her house. She'd feed Emily and then put her down for a nap in the crib she'd made up in her office. She could use the time to make calls to clients letting them know that she was back to care for their pets.

Miranda peeked out her office window as Dr. Gerrit De Van carted Mandy down the driveway headed for Clinton. As she nursed Emily, she took a scan of her life and instead of running away with her daughter and hiding from the world like she wanted to do, she summoned courage from deep down through the bottoms of her feet and pulled it all the way up through her body and into the sky. She'd figure out a way to make this difficult yet beautiful time in her life count and make it work. It was difficult because her husband had no part in Emily's life and wouldn't for three months. And beautiful because she held this soul that was her flesh and blood and the most precious treasure in her life.

Hank may not be a part of their lives right then, but she'd take one day at a time. Three months would go fast, and before she knew it, Hank would be back with them, and they'd be a happy family. Finally.

CHAPTER EIGHTEEN

That evening, the wind blew, shuffling lilac bushes as their branches scratched the windows of the main farmhouse. Inside, Justine was in jeans and sweatshirt and Richard in his usual polo shirt and khaki pants snuggled on the couch watching *The Golden Girls*. Justine admired how Blanche, Dorothy and Rose helped each other and yet lived their own lives, doing what they wanted to do. She identified with them as single women, losing their husbands to death or divorce.

When the show ended Richard ran a hand through his short salt-and-pepper dark brown hair, and said, "Those ladies are the ultimate bad girls." He smirked. "Don't you get any ideas."

Justine swung her head around and peered at Richard. "What do you mean?"

He scoffed. "They should act their age."

"And what would *that* look like? They're just having fun. I like them on the show." Justine grabbed their lemonade glasses and went into the kitchen. She stacked them in the dishwasher, closing the door with a thump.

Richard followed and leaned against the counter, folding his arms. "I can't believe you're upset with what I said. It's just a show."

"It may be just a show. But it's a show about women's issues and what can happen to women in their fifties when

80

they're alone. They're just trying to find their way. By saying they should act their ages it sounds like you think women should behave and keep in line." She began scrubbing the pan she'd fried bacon in earlier for their BLT sandwiches.

"The women make it look like they don't need a man in their life. It makes us feel insignificant."

Justine wheeled around and stood facing Richard. She tapped her finger on the kitchen table. "We need to have a talk. I'll make coffee and we can clear the air on some things."

Richard's eyes rolled and he let out a deep sigh. "What is it we need to discuss?" He pulled a chair out and begrudgingly sat down, watching Justine as she spooned coffee into the filter of the Mr. Coffee maker.

Thoughts of her beloved husband, Stanley came to mind. He would never have questioned her beliefs and wholeheartedly supported women's independence. She pushed a button and soon the brew's aroma swirled in the air.

Justine filled a mug for each of them and sat down. "You need to understand, Richard, that I'm self-sufficient and don't need a man in my life. That doesn't mean that I don't want to be with you. I do. But I have goals and dreams like any man might have wishes for his future."

He slouched for a few moments, staring at his coffee mug. Finally, he glimpsed at her and responded, "My marriage was different than yours, you already know that. My wife stayed at home, took care of our kids and the house. She didn't have a career or interest in doing anything else but being a homemaker. Far as I know. She never said anything, and we never talked about it. We just carried on in our roles, never questioning things as they were."

The coffee maker sputtered and hissed letting off steam.

"Justine, you're different. You're much stronger and fill your life with more activities than she did." He looked down again and circled his mug with his hands. "I'm supportive of you doing what you want to do. Like you, I was married a long time. It's an adjustment. That's all."

"It's an adjustment for me as well. Stanley and I had roles too." Stanley had always made her feel like an equal partner, sharing the work that kept their family and farm going. Justine took care of their home and bounty from the gardens and Stanley took care of the animals, crops, barn and outbuildings.

"It seems you're carrying out those roles even though he's no longer here."

A crease formed on her forehead. "What are you saying?"

"I'm saying that even though I'm in your life, you're living the same as when Stanley was alive. You continue to keep the farm going, living the farm life, growing vegetables and flowers, caring for the farm animals, keeping up this house. And you even have a job teaching in town. I'd like to know how you see us when we get married. Where will we live? What will our life look like?"

She took a few sips of coffee, and they sat quietly, the hum of the refrigerator in the background. "I guess since Emily was born, I hadn't thought about it."

His mouth turned into a frown. "I didn't think you had." He put his hand up. "I know it's special having a grandchild. I think I would be thrilled if one of my kids had children. But to be honest, I feel like our engagement has taken a back seat."

She folded her arms across her chest. "I know. And I'm sorry. But I'm not sorry for helping Miranda and her baby. With Hank's situation, she needs our help. I can't stop thinking when things are back to normal and he's home and they're a family, they won't need us so much. I just need you to be patient with the circumstances."

The muscles in his jaw twitched and he shifted his weight on the chair. "I have been. I've been very patient. And I'm a little irked that Hank could get into the situation he's in, in the first place. What kind of man gets into a bar fight? Don't you ever wonder about that, Justine? What kind of a son-in-law you have?"

"I'm mad at Hank too." Her jaw stiffened. "He's left my daughter in a bad situation. Not to mention the embarrassment of it all. But Hank is a good guy who made a bad decision a long time ago that's caught up to him. Yes. He should have taken care of it a couple years ago, but here we are. And I'm not going to leave my daughter now."

"I don't expect you to. But I need to ask when we're married where do you see us living?"

She didn't answer for a while as they sat and drank the last of their coffee. Quietly, Justine said, "Let's think about that when the time comes."

CHAPTER NINETEEN

Two states away, in Cheyenne, Wyoming, Hank sat on his bunk, shaved head in his hands. One week down and two months, three weeks left to go. How would he get through this? When he found out Miranda was pregnant last fall he was thrilled. He vowed to himself he would be a better father than his own and be there for his family and make his daughter feel loved.

And look how well that went. He was the same jerk as his own dad who abandoned his family when Hank was a boy and hadn't heard from him since. Hank had such high hopes for Miranda and their daughter. But what could he do without the freedom to grow and be the dad that Emily needed?

Would he ever get out of the doghouse with Miranda? He knew that she was disappointed in him. But could he ever be the man she deserved?

One good thing is he'd been moved to a different cell and had one bunk mate instead of three. His new bunk mate, Clyde, a chunky man in his fifties had been arrested for armed robbery. Not like his previous roomies. One of the guys Hank had been sharing a cell with reminded him of a weasel; sneaky and untrustworthy. The guy gave many excuses for beating his wife, evading responsibility. Hank couldn't stand it any longer.

When his new roomie, Clyde, woke up from his nap, he moved to the side of his bed. "What's got you down?" He gestured to the tray of food next to Hank, on *his* bed, untouched. "You want that? I ate all mine earlier but I'm still hungry."

Hank looked down at the tray of chipped beef, slimy spinach, canned peaches and store-bought cookies. He handed the tray to Clyde. "Knock yourself out."

As he watched Clyde devour the unpalatable food, a pressure cooker percolated inside of Hank as he focused on how to make it through the next three months without having an interior geyser bubble out of him and explode.

CHAPTER TWENTY

Nash leaned back, clasping hands behind his head in an old creaky swivel chair taking a moment to ponder his predicament. He took in the view of the Rockies out the window nestled above the Louis L'Amour westerns, his boss, Walt's, favorite that lined the top half of a bookshelf. Next to the window against the wall, a sofa that had been there for many years took up space, for occasional naps and overnights when a horse was close to foaling or Walt had been out riding for too long and didn't feel like going to the house for the night. Pictures of rodeo days lined the paneled walls, while old Carhartts and a cowboy hat hung on a coat rack in the corner.

Nash had been back to work in Wyoming a week. He'd promised Hank when he visited him in jail on his way back that he'd make sure Miranda had everything she needed. Nash wasn't happy about his friend's predicament, and he felt sorry for Miranda and what she had to put up with. It wasn't fair to her or their baby. But he was also loyal to his friendship with Hank. Nash didn't know how he'd manage working in Wyoming and looking after Miranda in Iowa, but he'd take care of things until Hank got out of jail.

Nash picked up the receiver of the black rotary phone from Walt's desk. As he dialed Miranda's number, he thought about what he'd say. She answered on the first ring.

"Hey, Miranda." Nash ran his hand over the black shadow on his face.

"Hi Nash. What a nice surprise."

Nash heard Emily fussing in the background. "Bad time?"

"She's just hungry. Amazing how often she eats. Pleasures of motherhood."

"Just checking in. How's it going?"

Miranda surveyed the scene in her clinic. All the cages were empty except for one where a cat was recovering from surgery. She had been back to work for two weeks and even though her practice was not even halfway to capacity she felt overwhelmed. Being a mother had taken a lot of energy and time. She had heard from women when she was pregnant that it changed your life, but she had no idea how much.

Miranda had vaccinated a litter of six-week-old Golden Retrievers, neutered a cat, dewormed three horses and filed down some sharp points in the mouths of two Shetland ponies in the last few days and she felt exhausted.

"Other than being tired all the time, things are alright."

Nash heard the weariness in her voice. But there wasn't much he could do about taking care of the baby. "How're things at the farm?"

"Mandy is ailing. Gerrit De Van has her at his clinic. Figuring out things. My cousin Larry is a big help with taking care of the animals."

Nash hesitated for a moment. "Tanya still there?"

"No. But Stephanie, Larry's daughter has begun working for me, helping in the clinic, taking care of the dogs and cats. She's also learning how to assist me with medical procedures. A big help."

"That's great. Glad to hear it."

"Nash?"

"Yeah?"

"Tanya called a couple days ago. She should be in Phoenix, Arizona about now, getting ready to compete in the

McDonald's Gymnastics Challenge." She chuckled softly. "Just in case you're wondering."

The skin on the back of his scalp prickled. "Thanks, Miranda. I'll leave you to it." He hung up the phone, picturing Tanya twirling in the air, dancing and stretching that cute, sexy tight body of hers. He thought about the last time they saw each other, out in the barnyard, just inches apart. Her breath softly caressed his face as he gazed into those warm brown eyes, sparkling in the sunlight. He'd been with other women. He'd even had a couple of serious relationships. What was it about Tanya that made him even more speechless than he already was? She could make his body buzz with anticipation when he saw her in the barn, grooming the horses, brushing their coats until they shone and the care she put into each one of those big animals. The time they rode together, laughing and talking about nothing. But, it meant everything to him. There was just something about her. He felt such a strong pull to see her, to be with her, that he felt light-headed. He brushed his hand over the back of his neck and rose from his chair just as his boss, Walt, stepped into the office.

"Hey, Nash. What's with the serious look, on a mission, like a cougar hot on a trail?"

Cattle bellowed in the nearby fenced area. "Can I talk to you about something?"

Walt leaned against the edge of the doorframe. He gestured. "Shoot."

Nash took a few moments to find the words. "There's this girl." He planted himself once again on the chair. "I can't stop thinking about her. We haven't been around each other all that much but the first time I met her, there was something special about her."

Walt folded his arms and crossed his ankles and waited for Nash to continue.

"I just have this ache right here." He put his hand on his chest. "Like the only thing that would cure it is to be near her."

"Sounds like you got it bad, my friend." Walt took a step toward Nash and wrapped his fingers around his shoulder and squeezed. "Looks like you need to go see a girl."

Nash looked up. "May take a few days."

"We're about done with branding and we won't move the cattle for a week or so once the weather turns. You got a few days comin' anyway."

"Thanks, Walt." Nash grabbed his Stetson, hurried out to the yard and hopped into his truck, stopping briefly by the bunkhouse to grab a few things before heading to Phoenix, Arizona.

CHAPTER TWENTY-ONE

*L*ate April, in Phoenix, Tanya warmed up for her competition at the McDonald's Challenge. The restaurant partnered with the Olympic Games and built a promotion around free food and medal counts. The more gold medals the United States won, the more food McDonald's gave away. Upon purchasing an item, a customer received a scratch-off card with an Olympic event on it. If the American team won gold in that event, the patron would get a free Big Mac. A silver medal, free french fries and so forth. It was called "When the US Wins, You Win" game. McDonald's would be a sponsor for the next five months until the Olympics in Seoul.

Tanya scanned the gymnasium and felt prickly heat on her feet, rising through her torso like a snake slithering to the top of her head as the pressure of the competition at hand seeped inside her mind. News teams stood, their cameras flashing, as they captured the day's events. Every move Tanya made that day would be recorded for the world to see.

She took some slow deep breaths trying to calm herself on the way to her warmup for floor exercise. But instead, her imagination took over and Nash popped into her thoughts as she leaped and twirled on the mat. His clear gray eyes gazed at her as if they were looking into her soul when she somersaulted in the air. When she moved to the beam to run through her routine his quiet presence and attentive nature steadied her on the beam during a back handspring. It could be dangerous, all these thoughts of him. She could lose her balance and fall. She had to get a grip. No more thoughts of Nash. She was here to compete. *Focus, Tanya. Focus.*

The gymnasts walked single file into the gym and stood still as the raw sound of the inspiring "Star-Spangled Banner" swelled and carried over the loudspeaker. The USSR team waited, and next, before the competition began, their emphatic and rousing anthem, "The Internationale" with a march-like pace resonated within the gymnasium. Large golden arches covered the surface of the wall separating spectators from athletes, McDonald's publicizing their sponsorship for the competition.

As the competition moved forward, Tanya waited, visualizing each flip, leap and turn. Excitement exuded from the crowd as they clapped to the rhythm of the music during the floor exercise competition. Flashes of camera lights flickered from the audience and newspeople.

When it was Tanya's turn to compete, she walked up to the floor exercise mat and glanced over to the edge of the gym and lost her focus. Was that really him? She rubbed her eyes and looked again. She had thought about him so much since she'd left Iowa that she didn't trust herself. Nash stood at the entrance, just inside the gym, watching her. She couldn't believe her eyes. She breathed deeply and gave her head a subtle shake.

Mentally, she joggled the sight of Nash away from her thoughts and approached the mat. And like she'd done hundreds of times before, shifted into competition mode.

After pirouettes, split jumps, leaps and flipping into back handsprings with piked double back somersaults, dancing to the dramatic battle theme of War/Fanfare from Rocky IV, Tanya threw her arms in the air finishing her routine. The power of the drumbeat, and brass cascaded through her as her chest swelled, feeling like she could conquer the world. She made her way back to her teammates and they hugged, celebrating her near perfect performance. Tanya glanced over to where she thought Nash had stood. But he was gone. Had he really been there? Or was that her imagination? The swoon she felt before her routine snuffled to a low simmer. Maybe her mind had played tricks on her. Tanya joined her teammates in encouraging the next competitor. "You'll do great. You got this!" She said, patting her teammate on the back.

CHAPTER TWENTY-TWO

Nash took one last look at Tanya with her team at the competition before he turned on his boot and headed for home. He wanted to stick around and see her after the competition, but Tanya was still with Daniel. It wasn't right for him to be presumptuous and think he even had a chance with her. Who was he to think she'd want to be with him? He was just a cowboy, not a fancy, elite athlete with bulging muscles and medals hanging around his neck. Nash's life was horses, cattle, and roaming the range.

He stepped into the warm spring air, the sky full of clouds. He noted that the mountain range looked different than the peaks in Wyoming. Not as high and brown. He searched for his truck and spotted Daniel hurrying across the parking lot. Nash froze, not wanting a confrontation with this jerk.

Daniel headed straight toward Nash, on his way to the entrance: three flags on poles high in the air flapped in the wind on a large cement plaza, a group of young girls clad in Phoenix Elementary t-shirts gathered on benches while a woman with a clipboard took roll call.

Daniel looked up and saw Nash. He stopped cold. "What are you doing here? Can't be for work. Last I knew your horse job was in Wyoming."

"None of your business."

"Quite a coincidence you'd be here when Tanya's here." Daniel came straight for him creating a barrier between Nash and the parking lot.

Nash tried to walk around him, but Daniel kept getting in his way. "Please, move."

Daniel moved a couple inches from Nash's face, teeth gritted and said, "You stay away from my girl."

"Last I knew, you couldn't own a person. She can be with whoever she wants."

Daniel took hold of Nash's flannel collar. "Don't mess with me."

Nash said, "Look pretty boy, I don't think you want to fight with me. I wrangle bulls that make you look like a small calf. You fight me, you're going to get hurt. Now wouldn't that wreck your precious career?"

Daniel let go and shoved Nash backwards as he steadied himself with a hop. Before he headed for his truck, Nash turned and said, "You're late. Competition's over. You missed Tanya." He then opened the door to his truck and got in. His wheels screeched as he left the parking lot and drove towards the highway.

For the next sixteen hours he contemplated how he would make it a priority to see Tanya again.

On the long bus ride home, Tanya thought about Daniel's promise to come see her compete. He'd told her he had a track meet the day before in Phoenix and said he'd stay an extra day so he could watch her routine. But then he never showed up. Maybe his coach made him return with the rest of the team.

Tanya's thoughts shifted to the mirage of Nash. Did she see him? Was he really there, or was it her fantasy getting the best of her? She closed her eyes, fell asleep and dreamed of Nash…

CHAPTER TWENTY-THREE

Back in Iowa, Miranda, posted at her clinic while she wrote bills and planned for the week ahead, answered the ringing phone. "Hello, Dr. Graaf."

"Miranda, Gerrit De Van here."

"Hi, Gerrit." Her heart pounded as she anticipated the news from Mandy's vet. "What'd you find out?"

"It *is* enterolithiasis. Do I have your permission to open her up and see what's stuck in her gut?"

Miranda felt a rush of heat in her face. She knew that surgery was risky, but she also wanted Mandy to get better. "You have my go ahead."

"Should be a straightforward procedure and her recovery should be brief." Kindness in his voice melted her fearful heart. "I'll take good care of her, Miranda."

Her horse was one of the most important beings in her life. Mandy had been with her through high school, college and more importantly she had been literally a shoulder to cry on throughout her dad's illness and afterwards when she grieved the loss of his death. Miranda had poured her heart out to Mandy, and she stood strong throughout it all. She desperately needed her horse to get well. She'd had too many changes in her life, with Hank going to jail and being a new mother and her own mother navigating a relationship with her new boyfriend, Miranda didn't know if she could handle one more loss. "Thank you, Gerrit. I appreciate your caring." Miranda was barely holding it together as it was.

This was another one of the moments in her life where she needed to reach down to her bootstraps, dig deep and find the courage to trust this new vet that she barely knew and have confidence that he'd take care of Mandy. She'd heard good things about him. He'd been practicing for ten years. He'd gone to the same university as her and was highly respected in the research community.

After all, Miranda was a mother now and had to step it up and be the mom Emily needed her to be. She swallowed the tears forming pools in her eyelids, took a deep breath and said, "Please let me know when you are out of surgery and how it went."

"Will do. Try not to worry."

After Miranda hung up the phone, she glanced at her sleeping baby in the portable crib, reached down and smoothed her hand over Emily's pink one-piece jammies. She crouched and gaped at the miracle breathing softly, the miracle that Miranda was responsible for, and a protective momma bear feeling surfaced. She'd do whatever it took to protect her baby and be the best mother she could be for Emily. The thought both terrified her and filled her with a powerful force that could move mountains.

Miranda heard footsteps approaching. Just then, Justine opened the clinic door and stepped inside. "Hi, honey. How's our little one?"

She rose from Emily's side and glanced at Justine. "How'd you do it, Mom?"

"Do what?"

"It's scary being responsible for a child. Their life depends on you."

"You just do what you have to do. You were number one with your dad and me. There was no question about that."

A line formed across Miranda's lips, and she crossed her arms in front of her. "I hope I can do as well as you can. You were a great mom to me. Still are."

Justine slid her arm around Miranda as they both gazed at Emily. "You will do just fine. You learn as you go." She squeezed her daughter. "Take one day at a time. Emily is lucky to have you for a mom."

Miranda leaned her head on Justine's shoulder and said, "Thanks, Mom."

"You may not see it now, but Emily is lucky to have Hank for a dad."

Miranda frowned.

"He'll come around. In a few months it will all be behind you."

"I hope so. I really do hope it will. It's a lot."

"Hank loves you. And you love Hank. Stuff happens in a marriage. It does to everyone that's married. You two have just gotten that stuff sooner than most."

Justine smiled and leaned to get a closer look at Emily. "And the best part of all is my sweet grandbaby. We're lucky to have this beautiful little baby in our lives. She's the bright spot in all that's going on."

"Don't forget that, Miranda. When you're in a dark space think of her."

"I get so focused on what's going wrong with Hank, and Mandy is now sick. I forget to count my blessings."

Justine turned to look at her. "What's wrong with Mandy?"

Miranda explained the surgery taking place in Clinton. "Gerrit De Van is taking care of her. It should go ok." A crease formed between her eyes. "He's supposed to be good and has a lot of experience in treating horses."

Justine placed a hand on Miranda's arm. "Sounds like she's in good hands. Try not to worry, honey."

"Seems since I became a mom it's all I do."

"Comes with the territory. Even when your kids grow up you still worry."

"Sorry for all that I put you through. Teenage years had to be hard."

Justine nudged Miranda. "It's all part of it. You have nothing to be sorry for."

CHAPTER TWENTY-FOUR

Later that afternoon, Larry dropped Stephanie off after school to help Miranda with the animals in the clinic. Miranda was in the middle of conducting lab tests for Ink, a black cocker spaniel that lived a couple of miles down the road. He was brought in by a family of six, four kids aged five to twelve and their parents. They had all crowded around the table while Miranda administered an exam. Ink wasn't eating or drinking water and presented with lethargy. Ink was a special member of the family, and they had worried looks on their faces. Miranda recommended that Ink stay with her, and she'd find out what was wrong. They each gave Ink a hug before they left their precious dog with Miranda. The five-year-old said through tears before they left, "Take cawe of my baby sista," adding more pressure to the situation.

Miranda looked up from the microscope to see Stephanie walking through the door. "Hi Steph. How was school?"

Stephanie, dressed in high-waisted jeans, baggy jean jacket with a bright orange scarf wrapped around her neck, tromped towards Miranda. Her plastic jellies squeaked on the cement floor. "Fine. I am *so* ready to graduate." She flipped her poofy, permed brown hair to one side of her brow.

"Just a couple weeks til then?" Miranda adjusted the knob on the microscope.

Stephanie nodded and took off her jacket and flipped it over a chair against the wall. "What do you want me to do today?"

"You can start by cleaning the animals' cages." A toy poodle whined and yipped in one of the cages. "And then take Muffy out for a walk." She smiled. "And, Stephanie, you might want to take that pretty scarf off. It'll get dirty, and you don't want it to get caught in one of the cages or one of the animals could grab hold of it."

Stephanie took her scarf and threw it on top of her jacket. She started with the cats' cages. There were three of them. One had been neutered, and his owner was picking him up in the morning. He was groggy and lifted his head when Stephanie came up to his cage. She stuck her hand inside and began stroking his soft gray fur. "Hi, there. You're such a sweety. Aren't you?" The cat licked her hand and then rolled his head back on the bottom of the cage. She wadded up a paper towel and moved gently around the cat, cleaning up any mess he may have made while recuperating from surgery.

Miranda watched as Stephanie went about cleaning the cage. "You're a natural with animals, Steph."

She grinned. "Thanks, Doc." Stephanie moved to the next cage and opened the door. The yellow tabby rubbed up against her arm.

"Animals know when someone is kind and good with them. They can sense good people."

"I've always liked animals. I was so sad when Beauty died last August."

"That was hard for me too."

"How do you do it?"

Miranda looked up from the slide she had in her hand.

"How do you do all the hard stuff, like putting down someone's pet?"

She eased the slide underneath the microscope lens and crossed her arms in front of herself. "That is absolutely the hardest part of my job. But it's part of what I do."

"I've always wanted to be a vet, but I don't know if I could do that."

"I didn't know that. How long?"

"Since I was a little girl." Stephanie looked at Miranda, then quickly back to the tabby snuggled in her arms. Her hand rubbed along the back of his silky fur.

"Stephanie, that's great."

She nodded, her face flushed.

"What's the matter?"

"I feel funny saying it out loud. It's been something I haven't talked about much. But ever since you went to vet school, I've thought about it. Then a couple years ago, when I learned you were my cousin, I thought how lucky that you were my cousin, the cool older girl in the family." Stephanie cleaned the bottom of the cage with one hand, still holding on to the cat with the other. When she finished cleaning, she placed the tabby back inside and latched the door on the cage.

Miranda came over to Stephanie and gently placed her hand on her shoulder. "Stephanie, I think it's great you want to do what I do." She smiled. "We can sure use more women in our profession. You'd be a gift to animals and the people who care for them."

Stephanie's eyes widened. "You mean it?"

Miranda nodded.

"I've never had anyone tell me that. I've always been good in science. Somehow knew I could take on the classes. But I've kept it to myself. I haven't even told my parents."

"Taking classes, this fall?"

"I'd like to but don't know what to do next."

"If you'd like, I can help."

Stephanie jumped a couple inches off the floor and her voice rose. "You'd do that? I thought you'd be too busy with the baby and everything."

"I'd *love* to mentor you."

She giggled. "Thank you."

"Maybe start by telling your parents."

"They know I like animals. My dad thinks I should go to school to be a vet tech."

Stephanie moved to the next cage and opened the latch. It was empty but needed cleaning. She sprayed disinfectant inside and started wiping it out. "But I don't know what they'd think about all the time and money it takes to be an actual vet."

"I can help you talk to them if you want."

"Would you?" The teen's face brightened. "That'd help a lot."

CHAPTER TWENTY-FIVE

A couple days later on a sunny spring day Miranda left Emily with Justine and drove her truck to Clinton, Iowa. Her trailer was already there because Gerrit had used it to take Mandy to his clinic. She pulled up the long driveway to his barn and parked in front. She got out of her truck and scanned the property, taking a view of four horses grazing in the large paddock. She noted the corral at which a woman was exercising a horse bandaged around his torso. It looked like someone had gotten generous with daffodil bulbs in the fall as the ground near the barn was covered with bright yellow posies. She headed toward the barn door, open for the day. Before she went inside, Gerrit exited the barn leading a large black and white Clydesdale.

"Wow. He's a beauty."

Gerrit's arm muscles rippled as he held tight the huge animal. Even for the strong and tall Dutchman, the horse was a handful. "He's a gentle giant."

Miranda went up to him and petted the white blaze on his soft face. "We had a draft horse in school, a black Percheron, that we treated. He had problems with hoof wall cracks. Four of us were assigned for his care. I grew fond of him and even though I was happy when he got better, and his owner got him, I was sad to see him go."

"You grow attached for sure. This guy, Tank, has been here for a couple weeks. Trying to sort his gut problems. I think I finally have figured it out. His owner has him as a pet and takes him on trail rides. Craziest thing."

"Soft ride."

"For sure. I'll take him out to the paddock. Let him graze a little and then we can go see Mandy. Walk with me."

They crossed the yard to the gate of the pasture. Miranda listened while Geritt talked about Mandy, describing the surgery. "She did well. I've done this procedure many times. She's strong. I think you'll be pleased at how she's doing."

Relief flooded Miranda from her head to her toes. She couldn't help herself and squeezed his arm. "Thank you, Gerrit."

He smiled and turned his head toward Miranda. "It's my pleasure."

They opened the gate and let the massive horse run free in the pasture, the white feathering on his feet blowing in the wind. They both stood and watched as he loped toward the center of the paddock, like a horse free from pain.

They chatted about the medical procedure he performed on the Clydesdale. Once they were inside the barn and headed toward Mandy's stall, Gerrit began telling Miranda about what he had to do with Mandy's surgery. "It's like I thought. There was a twine caught in her gut. Plus, there was a softball size calculi. If I hadn't taken the stone out, she wouldn't have made it. She was completely blocked."

When they reached Mandy's stall, Miranda rushed to the mare's side and hugged her, stroking her face. Mandy nickered and tucked her face into Miranda's chest.

"There's a bond between you two."

Miranda turned quickly and hugged Gerrit. "Thank you. Thank you."

Gerrit hesitated and then hugged her back. "You're welcome."

She pulled away, realizing she'd gotten affectionate with this man she hardly knew. "I am so grateful. I thought I might lose her." She wiped tears from her face.

As she looked at his clear blue eyes and his tan face, she couldn't help being drawn to him. He had saved the best friend she'd had much of her life. A girl and her horse. Nothing compared to that. With Hank gone she had a huge hole that needed filling. And if she'd lost Mandy, the hole would have become a cave. She was vulnerable and she knew it. *Be careful she told herself. Be careful. This man in front of you is handsome. Strong and helpful. Very helpful. But your guy is waiting for you. He'll be home soon. Or will he?*

They walked Mandy to the rig and Gerrit helped her put Mandy into the trailer and Miranda thanked him again. "Send me a bill."

"Professional courtesy. No charge."

She bent her head to one side. "At least for the meds."

"If I have a problem I can't solve with a dog or cat, I'll come to you for help."

She gave him a quick wave, got into her truck and left down the driveway.

CHAPTER TWENTY-SIX

Hank rode on the bus with five other inmates to their work site. They had been assigned to a ranch used for trauma survivors and physical therapy patients. The six were allowed to go offsite for work because they had lesser offenses. Hank's charge was a one off and the other guys were facing fraud and theft charges.

But that didn't mean they were nice to each other. Once they were settled in the barn with shovels, pitch forks, and wheelbarrows, Hank and the other guys got to work. However, one of them, Bennie Smith, was lazy. He'd stand with his arm on a shovel and talk while the other guys worked. This went on for a week and finally, a couple of the guys got tired of it. They conspired to get Bennie in trouble and tied him up and put him inside a stall.

One day, Bennie was left all day while the guys worked. Hank didn't want anything to do with their plan. He and two other guys kept working in the huge barn housing several horses. The guys shoveled manure and old straw into a wheelbarrow and pushed it out onto a huge pile in the barnyard again and again. Bennie had fallen asleep.

When it came time for the bus to take them back at the end of the day, Hank and the rest of the men got onto the bus.

The bus driver did a head count. "Where's Smith?"

The guys shrugged. Soon yelling erupted from the inside of the barn and the driver hustled toward the noise. Within a few minutes the driver and Smith headed for the bus and got on.

The bus driver stood as the six guys stared straight ahead. "Who's responsible for tying Smith up?"

Hank was caught between a rock and a hard place. He knew if he had untied Bennie or told on the guys, they'd have called him a nark, but not doing anything once the bus driver realized he only had five guys they'd all get in trouble. Hank's time in jail would be extended. This was one of the many difficult things about jail. You tried to keep your nose clean, and keep your mouth shut and you still got into trouble. It was often a no-win situation.

"We're not going anywhere until someone fesses up."

Hank noticed one of the guys sitting behind Smith poking his finger hard at the back of his neck out of view of the driver.

Smith blurted, "It's my fault. Don't blame the guys."

The driver raised his eyebrow. "You tied yourself up?"

The guy behind Smith jabbed harder. "Yep, I did."

The driver shook his head. "Your funeral." He sat down and backed the bus out of the designated parking area and drove back to the jail.

When they arrived, Hank noticed the driver talking to the jail supervisor. The thought that this one incident would come to bite them all kept nagging him. He'd deal with that later if something happened. But he'd have to do what he could and continue to be on his best behavior even if it meant looking the other way when rules were broken. Minding his own business, staying alert at all times, and trusting no one were *his* rules for getting out of jail as soon as possible. Hank planned on working hard and getting along with other inmates even if he didn't like them.

CHAPTER TWENTY-SEVEN

Back at the farm, Justine and Richard worked in the garden planting green beans, beets, cantaloupe and carrots on a cool May morning, so cool that Justine had her winter jacket on. She took her gloves off and whistled while she fiddled with the packages of seeds.

Richard dug holes with a trowel. His face scowled and he pulled his wool hat down further on his head. "Why do we have to plant when it's so cold outside?"

"You'll be happy when there's fresh vegetables throughout the summer."

"They do have produce at the store, you know?" He plunged a small shovel into the earth. "Or the market, you can buy food there too."

Justine *tsked* and threw him a look. "It's not the same as growing your own."

"You know, when we're living in Chicago after we're married, there won't be room for a garden at my house. You'll be a lady of leisure and buy vegetables at the grocery a mile down the road."

She paused mid-tear on the package of carrot seeds. "Living at your house? When did we decide that?"

"I figured that when Hank is out of jail, back home, you'd be ready to get on with our lives."

She set the package of carrot seeds on the ground and glared at Richard. "Why are you making decisions without me?"

He back peddled. "I just thought…I hadn't firmed up that decision."

"But that's what you want, isn't it?"

"Well…" He squirmed like a worm wiggling out of a log onto the dirt.

"Be honest. You want me to start up a new life with you in Chicago. Forget everything I love here in Iowa. And make it all about us?" Her hands went to her hips. "About you."

"I just want to make your life easier. I have that to offer you. I know it's different than how you've lived. But you deserve a life of leisure. You're an amazing woman. I love you. I want to give you more."

She sat on the ground; hands wrapped around her folded legs and looked out over the farm: The Brown's had finished planting a hundred acres of corn for them a few days prior. The Graaf's five horses flicked their tails as they grazed on the peaceful pastureland. Memories of Stanley and Justine walking hand in hand on their property, enjoying picnic dinners and sunsets danced through her mind.

Silence enveloped Justine and Richard.

Justine considered Richard's words for a few moments and then cut her arm through the icy May air like a lift arm on a tractor. "What about my job? I just started teaching again after all these years."

"You don't have to work anymore with me. We don't need the money."

She fixated on the black earth, the earth that grounded her. "But I want to be a teacher. I've put it off for many years, working this farm."

"You can put it all behind you, Justine." Richard reached out, barely grazing her hand. His face turned solemn, and he studied her. "You don't want to give it up do you?"

Justine shook her head slowly. "I once thought I gave my life up for the family that went back generations. But little by little I learned to love it. It grew on me. I became a part of it. And it became more than being married to Stanley and living this life with him. His family became my family and now that I have a granddaughter, it's part of her too. The earth has become more solid than ever."

"And teaching?"

"That's a dream I've had for a long time. I'm now finally living out that dream, this late in life. But it's happening. I am blessed to have everything that I want." She smiled at him. "And now I have you too."

He sat in the dirt beside her. "I don't know if I can live on a farm like you'd want me to." He took her hand. "I want a wife that doesn't have to work. I take pride in giving you things that you have never had. And it fills me up knowing that you are doted on and don't have to do a thing."

She slowly took her hand back and placed it in her lap. "I love you. But the life you want…That's not me, Richard. I have dreams and I want to make the most of the years that I have left. It may be later in life, but I want to make it happen. If I can't live out my dreams and do the things I have passion for…"

"You won't be happy?"

"As much as what you're offering is amazing, it's just not for me. I would grow to resent it. And I'd resent you. I don't want to get to that point."

"What are you telling me?…Are you breaking up with me?"

Justine nodded slowly. The weight in her stomach felt like she'd swallowed a ball of yarn, the murkiness scraping along the insides of her belly.

Richard put down the trowel, kissed her quickly on her cheek and stood. He wiped the dirt from his knees and the seat of his pants.

She watched him open the back door to the house as she sat in the dirt. A few minutes later, he came outside with a suitcase in his hand. He waved and then got into his Cadillac and drove down the driveway, leaving dust behind. The last she'd see of Richard.

The tightness of the ball of yarn in her belly unraveled and bit by bit was swept away by the cool breeze in the air. The sun came out and shone on the seedlings of lettuce, spinach and radishes, warming the air that had felt cold for too long.

CHAPTER TWENTY-EIGHT

A couple days after Richard had left, Miranda and Justine sat at Justine's kitchen table, Emily cradled in Justine's arms. She looked at her grandchild. "I'm fine, Miranda. Really. It was for the best. I'm sad because Richard's not in my life, but it just wasn't going to work. My life is here with you and Emily."

"I just want you to be happy, Mom. We could have made it work, travel to Chicago to see you. It's not that far away. Only a few hours."

"I want to see Emily every day, watch her grow up. When she learns how to walk and the first time she says, grandma." Justine's eyes glowed when she fixed her gaze on her first and only grandchild. "She needs her grandma, yes, she does, don't you, Emily?" Justine smiled brightly. "You are such a sweety. You are."

"Richard and I didn't get along the best, but I would have tried for you, whatever you needed."

Justine put her hand on Miranda's cradling a cup of tea. "I know that dear, but actually, I feel freer than ever, able to completely be me and not stifled by someone who didn't support my dreams." She squeezed her daughter's arm, then let go. "I love teaching, and I love living here on our farm. I love everything about it. The uncertainty of the weather affecting the crops, the hardships when a storm comes and ruins our acres of soybeans." She took Emily's hand in hers and caressed her tiny fingers. "It's in my blood now. Your dad is gone but he left me with his family's heritage, and I feel honored that I can keep it going. And now that our family is growing, I want to pass it on to Emily."

"That's generous of you, Mom." Miranda drank tea and looked at her mom over the rim of her mug. "What if Emily doesn't want anything to do with farming? I wouldn't want you to give up everything and it didn't turn out the way you'd planned."

"I can't control the future. But I know that I love where I am. Here at the farm. The rest will take care of itself." Justine shifted her gaze to the kitchen window. "Who's that in the black dually?"

Miranda turned to look. "Oh." Her face brightened. "That's Gerrit's truck."

Justine noticed the perk seeing Gerrit gave her daughter. "The vet? What's he doing here?"

"Let's go find out."

Both women trekked toward the barn, Justine beside Miranda, carrying Emily.

Gerrit turned and approached Miranda at the driver's side of his truck. "Hi ladies. Miranda, I hope I'm not overstepping, but I have a patient that I could use your help with. I've got him in the back seat. He's just not getting better."

Miranda smiled and gestured. "This is my mom, Justine."

Gerrit and Justine shook hands. "Nice to meet you, Justine. Your daughter has a way with animals."

Justine smiled. "Always has had."

Miranda said, "I'd love to help. Who do we have with you?"

Gerrit opened the back passenger door. He scooped up a golden retriever and held him so Miranda could see. "This is Lucky."

"Bring him into the clinic."

Gerrit followed Miranda inside and laid him on an exam table. "He's been whimpering a lot and avoiding going for walks, his favorite thing, for a couple weeks. Something his owner and him have enjoyed a couple times a day. She's an older woman, a widow, and this is her only companion at home and she's worried about him. I really want to help but can't seem to find what this big guy needs."

Justine followed them inside the clinic, observing Miranda interacting with this tall, blond vet with big muscles and a charming smile. *She'd better be careful. Danger! Danger!* She continued watching as they huddled, a few inches from each other, their hands moving together like a synchronized dance palpating the dogs' back, legs and belly. Justine realized Gerrit was interested in Miranda. He could figure out how to treat this dog. Justine was no vet but come on, it couldn't be that hard. She smirked slightly. He was here to get Miranda's attention.

And Miranda was getting hooked, line, and sinker. Just then, the door opened and in walked Stephanie and Larry. Whew. Saved by the cousins.

Glad there was a buffer and distraction, Justine said, "Miranda, I'll take Emily to your house for a nap. Hi Larry. Stephanie." She bustled toward the door, Emily in her arms.

"Thanks, Mom," Miranda said, a puzzled look on her face as she watched Justine leave. Miranda smiled at the newcomers. "Hi, guys. Larry, thanks for dropping Stephanie off. She's such a big help and she learns fast too." She winked at Stephanie. "Next thing you know she'll be assisting me in procedures with animals, even surgery."

"I told her I think she should go to Scott Community College for the vet tech degree, and she could get a job quickly. They've got a certificate, I think, only a year."

Miranda and Stephanie exchanged a look. Miranda realized it was going to be hard convincing him that his daughter could go further in school. She was smart and had a natural gift with animals. Stephanie reminded Miranda of herself when she was a girl. In time she'd have to talk with her cousin, open his mind to the possibilities and not limit his daughter's future.

The big golden stood and his four limbs slipped and slid on the metal surface of the table. Miranda gently took his collar in one hand and stroked his back with the other. "Let's get him on his side and I can evaluate what's going on with him."

Gerrit on one side of the table, and Miranda on the other, took hold of his chest, abdomen, and backend and placed the large dog on his side.

She listened to his heart, palpated his abdomen, and then she looked at each of his paws. When she checked one of the back paws, she noticed redness and puffiness on his pad. "Well, what do we have here, Lucky?"

Gerrit held the dog's head, while he whimpered as Miranda spread his big paw apart. "I can see why you're becoming popular with dog owners in the area."

Miranda glanced sideways. "That means a lot coming from you." Miranda looked through a magnifying glass for a close examination, took some tweezers and plucked a thorn tucked in the inside of one of Lucky's nails. "I could hardly see this. Looks like a barberry thorn." She raised the tweezers to show Gerrit.

"How did I miss that? No wonder he's been ornery and hasn't wanted to go on their usual daily walks."

She rubbed some antibiotic ointment on Lucky's foot and then dabbed some pain medication on it too. "Should feel better now." She petted Lucky's head, and his big brown eyes glowed with gratitude.

Gerrit scooped up the big dog and placed him gently on the floor. Lucky shook and began panting. He plunked his front paw on Miranda's leg. It looked like he was smiling at her, thanking her for taking out the thorn that had been hurting him.

She rubbed his big head. "Probably all he could think about was that thorn. Stephanie, why don't you take Lucky out for a walk."

Stephanie jumped up from a chair beside the desk. "Love to." She scooped the dog's leash from Miranda and led him outside.

Gerrit leaned against the exam table, hooked one foot over the other and placed a hand on Miranda's shoulder. "Thanks, for your help."

Miranda looked up at the tall Dutchman, his blue eyes flickering as he smiled at her, and then removed his hand. A flash of lightning danced through her body, and she squeezed the end of the table to steady herself. Her lips parted and she found herself speechless, her face simmering as an uncomfortable feeling slithered through her belly. It had been a month since she'd felt Hank's touch, and she didn't like how her body betrayed her when Gerrit reached out moments earlier. She couldn't allow herself to succumb to his charm and good looks. From now on, she'd keep herself in check.

Just then, they heard a yelp in the barnyard. They ran out to see what the commotion was. Stephanie held her hand upright, blood trickling down her arm. Larry came running from inside the barn, holding a hoof pick.

Lucky ran through the barren corn field, ears flapping and leash dragging behind him. Gerrit sprinted, chasing him, trying to catch up to him. He called out.

Miranda went to Stephanie holding her arm. Miranda asked, "What happened?"

Larry crouched beside them and gaped at his daughter.

"He bit me. We were walking, things were going great." She sniffled. "He cried out. I bent to see what had happened and took his paw, thinking it was the one he hurt before, and he bit me just like that. He was fine one minute and then the next … She sucked in air. "Ouch."

"Come on in, and I'll clean up your bite."

Larry perched in a chair nearby as he watched Miranda treating Stephanie. She cleaned up the wound with an antibiotic and examined the bite. "I don't think you'll need stitches, but he gave you quite the cut. I'll wrap it up and it should be as good as new." She took out a sterile bandage and spread it over the wound, securing it with tape. "Keep this clean while it heals." She took a bottle from her purse and shook two white pills into her hand. "Here's some aspirin to help with the pain."

Miranda watched her as Stephanie swallowed the pills. "I'm sorry this happened, Stephanie. Animals can be unpredictable. I've been bitten a few times. By a couple dogs and a cat bit and scratched me pretty good." She grimaced. "It's part of the territory."

Stephanie sat in silence while she gathered her thoughts and her face paled. "I don't feel well. I want to go home."

Larry got up from his chair. "I'll drive her home."

"Larry?"

Miranda gathered the bandages and ointment. "Getting bit is a shock." She smiled slightly. "Have her take it easy."

Before they left, Larry said, "We'll call you later."

Miranda remembered that Gerrit was outside chasing down Lucky. She grabbed a jacket from the coat rack and headed toward the corn field. Across the field she saw Gerrit, leading the big Golden by his side. Miranda walked toward them and within minutes she met up with him.

Gerrit said, "I ran over to the neighbor's yard. He was playing with a donkey." Shook his head. "Craziest thing, never seen a donkey and a dog taking such a liking to each other."

Miranda laughed. "My dog Ben and that donkey have been friends for years. Good thing Ben is inside right now, or he might be jealous of Petey's new friend."

"Petey's the donkey?" They continued walking, flickers of heat from Gerrit's touch earlier in the clinic sparked between them.

Miranda felt Gerrit's eyes on her, but her heart whispered a warning. As they strolled, she kept her gaze looking straight ahead. "I really appreciate what you did for Mandy. She's acting like her normal self now. With all that's going on, you don't know what a relief it is to have my horse feeling better. I feared I might lose her."

"I heard your husband is in jail?"

Miranda knew that Dutch people could be blunt and say whatever was on their mind, much as her grandparents once did, so she was told. But she still felt a jolt from his comment. "Yeah. He is." Stunned that he knew this information she looked at him. "Where did you hear that?"

"Just gossip from a farrier that comes to my clinic."

It was going to be hard to keep news about Hank contained to the farm. Miranda's mouth took over, and she started talking even though she felt it was too much information to share with someone she hardly knew but she felt compelled to share more. "It's something that could have been prevented. He's feeling bad about what happened and how it's put me and Emily in a rough situation. But I think it's harder on him, missing out on seeing Emily grow and change. Although it's been tough on me too."

They reached the barnyard and Gerrit stopped by his truck. He turned to look at Miranda. His clear blue eyes had kindness in them. She had a flash back to when she was struggling with her dad's illness and when her old boyfriend, Dylan, had cheated on her. When she'd first met Hank in Farm and Fleet, she had spilled and told him about her pain then. Hank's eyes looked kind like Gerrit's did right then. Caring in them. And wanting to help. She drew in a breath.

"Thanks for helping with Lucky. Feeling kind of stupid, I didn't see it myself." He picked up the big dog and let him hop into the back, watching him curl around and lie down on the back seat. Gerrit said, "If there's anything I can do to help, just holler."

Miranda watched as Gerrit drove his rig down the driveway. He was a nice guy, and she was confused about the feelings that were beginning to germinate when she thought about him. She held her elbow while the opposite hand made a fist against her mouth as the dust rolled behind his vehicle.

CHAPTER TWENTY-NINE

A couple weeks later, Miranda drove Justine's station wagon along I-80 on a warm May morning as they headed once again for Cheyenne, Wyoming. They were going to see Hank. Wild irises shouted their blue and purple colors lining the side of the freeway. It'd been three weeks since Miranda had seen her husband. And three weeks since he'd seen Emily. Their daughter slept in the car seat in the back seat.

Justine turned and glanced at her granddaughter. "She's so adorable when she's sleeping. Looks so peaceful. I'd sit in a chair and stare at you when you were a baby, watch you sleep."

"That's sweet, Mom." Miranda smiled, her hands tight on the steering wheel. "I do the same. I look at her and think I'm so blessed to have this little miracle given to me. Tears come to my eyes when I think of the responsibility it is to raise a child. When they're a baby, they are completely depended on you to survive."

"It's daunting, for sure."

"I always question whether I'm doing a good enough job. Am I making any mistakes that will permanently scar her for life?"

Justine wrapped her fingers around Miranda's shoulder. "You're a good mom, honey. Doing great."

Miranda glanced at her mom. "Thanks, Mom. That means a lot, especially coming from you."

They sat in silence for a few minutes.

"I also worry that Hank missing out on the first months of Emily's life will affect her."

"She'll be fine." Justine turned her head and studied her daughter. "Just be mindful about how *you're* doing without Hank. I imagine it can be lonely without him."

Miranda's heart pounded and her mouth became dry. "What is *that* supposed to mean?"

"I know Gerrit has been helping you but be careful. He's a charming, handsome man."

"He's just a colleague, Mom." It was as if Miranda's conflicted feelings about Gerrit had been written on the side of their barn for her mom to see."

"Just be careful, honey."

Miranda gripped the wheel and tried steadying herself, taking in slow quiet breaths. Her mom was overreacting. She had it all under control. Gerrit was just a colleague. Nothing more.

After several minutes, Justine said, "I know you love Hank, and I know you're committed to him. I didn't mean to upset you. And Emily will do just fine. Kids are resilient. Life isn't perfect for any of us. But if you have parents that love you and do the best they can and are lucky enough to have two loving parents, you'll do ok. And you and Hank both have a lot of love to give Emily. Enjoy these early days, they go so fast. They seem long now, but it flies by, believe me. It goes faster the older they get. It did for me with you."

Miranda's defense softened and her teeth peeked through lips in a thin smile. "If I'm half as good as you as a mom…"

Several hours passed, after gas and food stops, and breaks to feed Emily. Miranda turned her signal on and drove off the freeway onto the exit leading to Cheyenne and journeyed through the city leading to the governmental center and jail.

Before they went inside, Miranda fed Emily, changed her, and then wrapped her into a blanket onesie to keep her warm in air cooler than Iowa had been.

Three generations of Graafs headed toward the main doors of the jail. Justine said to Miranda, "I'm going to wait outside for you, honey." She turned and walked toward a picnic table that perched under an elm tree. On the sidewalk, a wiry man in a cowboy hat and boots walked toward her. He tipped his hat. "Ma'am." He slowed his pace and eyed her for a moment. "Didn't I see you at Hank Driskill's hearing?"

Justine hesitated, eyeing his weathered tan face and then said, "Yes. And you are?"

"Walt. I'm Hank's old boss."

She reached her hand out. "I'm, Justine Graaf, Hank's mother-in-law."

He took her hand. "Very nice to meet you, Ma'am."

"So, polite here in Wyoming." Still shaking hands. "You can call me Justine." His hands were strong and rough from years of hard labor, yet he held her hand gently in his. He had a calm steady nature and seemed like a man who wouldn't be shaken by much.

"Tough break, for Hank."

"Bad timing."

"Nash tells me he's got a little one."

"Just six weeks old, their Emily."

"Well, I'd better get. Nice to meet you, Justine."

"I'm glad you're here for him, Walt."

Walt tipped his hat, then hesitated. "Hank's a good guy, Justine. Don't give up on him. He'll more than make up for his mistakes. The only reason he's in here is he tried to help someone." He turned and Justine watched the cowboy, as he walked away.

Miranda went inside heavy wooden doors to the front desk of the jail; a solid metal counter, cluttered with paperwork, forming a barrier between the officers and visitors. She stepped to the tall workstation and said, "I'm here to see Hank Driskill." A woman handed her a clip board and had her sign in.

Within a few minutes Miranda was led to the booth where she'd seen Hank the last time she visited him. She settled in and took off Emily's blanket sleeper. The baby's little face was sweaty from the warmth, and Miranda swiped her thick blond hair sticking to her forehead.

After a long wait, Hank entered the opposing booth and sat down. Miranda noted he looked haggard, like he'd lost weight. There was a bruise above one of his eyes. "Hi babe."

"Are you ok? Did you get into a fight?

Hank tugged on the collar of his jumpsuit and scratched his neck. He didn't want to tell her about the fight he got into defending himself when a guy jumped him on his way back from work release. He was headed into his cell. The guy came from behind and grabbed his arm demanding money that he might have received while he was out. Hank jerked away from him and the guy punched him in the eye.

Avoiding Miranda's question, he peered at Emily. "She's grown." He looked at Miranda with sad eyes. "I've missed you. It's been three weeks."

"I miss you too. It's been hard. Lots goin' on with the baby and the farm. Lots to take care of. But Larry's helping. So is Stephanie." She rattled on. "Mandy was sick, and I couldn't figure it out. I had a vet from Clinton come see her. Gerrit De Van." She felt her face get red. "I think he may have saved her life." She said once again, nerves in her voice, "I just couldn't figure it out. But *he* did." She fixed a stare at Emily and her eyes held there. She took her daughter's little fingers inside her own.

Hank said, "What aren't you telling me, Miranda?"

"Nothing. It's just been hard, is all. It's a lot to bring Emily and come here."

"You have feelings for this guy?"

Miranda jerked her head upwards. "No. Of course not. I was worried about Mandy. I would have been devastated had I lost her."

They sat in silence for a while.

"Babe. I love you. I feel helpless here. When I get out, I'm going to make it up to you and Emily. Big time."

She put her hand on the glass. "I love you too. I know you're sorry for everything. I wish you were out of here, too. What happened to your eye?"

"You gotta stick up for yourself in here. There's a pecking order."

An officer came up behind Hank. "Time to go back, Driskill."

Hank looked at her with pleading eyes. "Wait for me, babe." He pressed his hand to the plexiglass. "Please wait."

Miranda had never seen Hank this way, desperate. He looked so sad and defeated, like a trapped animal in a cage, at the mercy of the people nearby to give him food or let him out for fresh air. Suddenly, her anger at him turned to sadness. He was such a great guy and locked up, all his power had been taken away. Freedom was so valuable. It had become more apparent now than ever. She had never had to realize how lucky she was to be free. Free to do what she wanted. Free to live a life she had passion for. She was determined to do what she could to help Hank by being strong and taking care of their daughter, her practice, their home and the farm.

On their drive home Justine and Miranda rode in silence for the first hour, deep in their own thoughts. Miranda thought about her conversation with Hank. She couldn't believe he asked her if she had feelings for Gerrit. Of course she didn't. The vet was just helping out is all. What else was she supposed to do? Her horse was suffering. She had to get someone to help.

Finally, Justine said, "I saw Hank's boss, Walt."

Miranda jerked as her thoughts were interrupted.

"You, ok?

Miranda nodded. "Just deep in thought."

Justine prattled on. "He seemed like a nice man. He was there to see Hank. Seemed almost fatherly to him."

Miranda's thoughts about Gerrit and Hank's question settled in her belly and stayed there. "Hank hasn't seen his dad since he was a boy."

"I remember you telling me that when you first started dating." Justine looked at Miranda, whose eyes focused on the road. "How *is* Hank?"

"Not too good. He seemed so sad, desperate almost. And trapped."

"It can't be easy for him. Miranda, it's important that you don't give up on him."

She flashed her mom a look. "Why would you say that? Of course I'm not giving up on him."

"It's just that…that vet, Dr. De Van."

Her body felt hot, the fire growing like she'd been caught in the act of doing something wrong. "That again?"

"The look on your face the other day when you were helping that Golden on the exam table in your clinic. You were huddled, working on something together."

She rolled her eyes. "I thought we were done with this conversation on the way to Wyoming." Her voice rose. "Hank's only been gone a month. I'm not that fickle that I'd fall for another man."

"Well, you *are* vulnerable. You've just had a baby. And without Hank here to support you and be the dad, I'm just worried that you'll be swept off your feet."

She thumped her hand on the steering wheel. "I can't believe you'd think that I'd be that disloyal. I love Hank." Miranda felt like she was in fifth grade in trouble with her mother for cheating on a test at school.

"You have a lot in common with the vet, same profession. People can bond while working on a project together. Like doctors working on difficult cases. Just be careful." Justine looked out the window, staring at the rolling hills and grazing land.

Miranda ground her teeth, flexed her fingers on the steering wheel and forged ahead, anxious to get home and back to her own space, away from the strain of hearing Justine's words.

CHAPTER THIRTY

Hank was taken back to his cell. On the way down the corridor, he noticed all the men in their cells, like caged animals, unfit to be out in society. He was one of those men. He didn't want to be, but he was, nonetheless. His heart ached when he'd seen Miranda and Emily, his family, that'd he'd not been a part of the last several weeks. What was he going to do? How would he get past this?

Miranda obviously had feelings for that vet back home. Why did *her* horse have to get sick? Usually, Miranda could figure out ailments, especially with horses. She had a gift when it came to working with horses and treating them. Why did it have to happen that she couldn't figure out what was wrong with her own horse? Bad timing, it was. Once in his cell Hank sat on the bed and rubbed his hands down his face.

His cellmate, Clyde, said, "What's got you shook up?" His double chin shifted and jiggled as he talked. "Your woman ditch you?"

Hank looked up, gritted his teeth, "Don't mess with me, I'm not in the mood."

He swung around and stretched out on his four-inch thick mattress and closed his eyes. The thought of Miranda with another man made him feel sick. It couldn't happen. It wouldn't happen. But who was he fooling? He was in here and that guy was out there, living his life. And working with his wife. Plus, he was an educated guy that had similar interests to Miranda. They had veterinarian medicine in common.

What did Hank have to offer? He wasn't educated like that guy. He didn't have some fancy degree from some fancy university. He didn't know about "itis" this and "osis" that. He didn't know how to operate on an animal. He could train a horse, wrangle cows, take care of horses' and cows' hooves but he didn't know what to do if the animals got sick. The fear in him that he could lose his family or his marriage to Miranda roared through his body like a mad bull that was headed straight for him. Would they make it through all this?

After moments with his crooked arm over his eyes, Hank rolled to his hands and knees on the floor and succumbed to doing pushups. One, two, three, twenty, twenty-five…he'd do what he could, and that started with getting stronger, at least on the outside. The inside would take work. There was a library available to inmates. He would read every book he could get his hands on. Maybe he wouldn't have a fancy degree, but he'd be educated and learn as much as his brain would take in before he got out.

Hank stood, pressed his hands against the cell bars in a hamstring stretch and watched a guard, Mr. Johnson quietly hand something to an inmate, a couple cells down from him. The inmate was the same bully who told Hank he had assaulted his wife when Hank first arrived. The guard nodded and left. Hank found it odd, but jail was full of strange moments. The inmate closed his hand, gritted his teeth and pounded his fist in the air toward Hank. Hank went back to the floor and did more pushups.

CHAPTER THIRTY-ONE

As Hank was swirling from emotions about Miranda, Tanya swirled from preoccupation about a certain guy she couldn't seem to shake from her mind. On the bus headed back from Arizona to Colorado Springs, Tanya and her teammates were resting and mentally preparing for the next competition. Most of the girls were napping but instead of mentally going over her routines on the beam and floor exercise which she did every waking hour, Tanya was distracted by thoughts of Nash. Why did he stick to her mind like a perfect landing after a beam dismount? The more she tried to think of her routine, the scenery outside, as they passed trees, cactuses and rocky terrain, oh and Daniel, the more she thought about Nash and his clear gray eyes that stirred a warm glow deep inside. His cowboy silent type gave her a feeling of solid rock yet buzzing excitement she couldn't shake off. She hardly knew him. They'd only been together working on the Graaf farm a few times, helping out. But there was that one time he sat with her, keeping quiet, letting her feel less alone, like someone really cared, without saying a darn thing. It meant the world to her. He hadn't told her what to do. He just let her be. It was such an all-encompassing, acceptance of all of her. No guy had ever done that for her.

Daniel could be caring at times. He understood her dream of being an Olympian. No one else understood that like he did. But what would they do after the Olympics? Did they have anything else in their relationship? Their whole life was competing, fine-tuning their sports. It wasn't an easy life. Not many could understand what it took to be an elite athlete. They supported each other's athletic goals.

So why did her thoughts always start on one road and then take a detour down Nash Road?

The bus driver finally parked at the entrance to the hotel they'd be staying in for one night before continuing their journey back home. They grabbed their stuff, following the gymnastics coach into the lobby. Their competition schedule was stringent. They needed all these chances so they could reach beyond and improve their skills each time. Tanya was focused on the gold, and she thought this might be her last opportunity to compete in the Olympics. A gymnast was considered old once she was in her mid-twenties, like Tanya. She wanted to be the best she could possibly be and with that dream hopefully win the gold medal.

CHAPTER THIRTY-TWO

Thirty miles from Cheyenne, Wyoming Nash thought about Tanya as he rode his black horse and wrangled cattle with two other cowboys and his boss, Walt. The wind blew across the wide-open plains, as usual. The soft golden light from the sunrise cast images on the Laramie Mountains in the distance. The wide-open spaces of the range gave Nash a sense of peace and satisfaction that this is what he did for a living. He lived most of his days outdoors. But underneath that peace was a stirring. A yearning that wouldn't go away and in fact got stronger and stronger as time went by. He tried to rid himself of thoughts of that one spicy, athletic gymnast that had hooked him from the moment he saw her in his buddy, Hank's driveway.

When Tanya stepped out of the car a few months back in her USA gymnastics warmup suit, Nash was a goner. Her dark brown eyes that warmed his heart the moment he was introduced and her great sense of humor and toned petite body took his breath away.

The more he tried to think of other things and told himself she was out of his league, the more he wanted her and fantasized about them together. Who was he kidding? She was in a relationship with an Olympian. Tanya wouldn't be interested in Nash. He was just a cowboy. A simple guy that liked simple things. He didn't need much. And up until then he didn't think he wanted anything serious. This had never happened to him before. He'd dated. Had a couple long-term relationships. But the women he dated often got tired of his lifestyle. He worked long hours, breaking horses and handling cattle and sometimes he'd be gone for days at a time. The ranch life was hard. But mostly there'd never been anyone that grabbed his attention like Tanya. She was someone special.

Nash pressed his thighs against his black gelding's sides urging him forward, heading toward a stray calf that bolted away from the herd. Horse and rider galloped in front of the small Hereford and the baby trotted back to his mother.

He scanned the other heads of cattle and thought about the time he and Tanya helped the Graafs'. He felt a spark then and knew she felt it too. He could see it in her eyes. That time she was upset and he just sat with her. He wanted to wrap his arms around her and let her melt into him, but instinct told him just to let her be. Let her feel what she needed to feel. Her boyfriend, Daniel, was so demanding and controlling. The last thing a strong and capable woman like Tanya needed was someone to tell her what to do. She could make her own decisions and live her own life. At that time in the barn, he just wanted to be that soft place for her to fall.

But they lived different lives and lived in different states. Would their connection be enough to make it work between them?

The whistles and "yip yips" from the other cowboys stole his attention from his deeper thoughts. "Kai." He urged his big black gelding toward a stray calf veering from the herd. Right then, he had to focus on his work. He'd think about Tanya later.

CHAPTER THIRTY-THREE

Once their bus rolled into the Colorado Springs athletic training center, two days after the Phoenix competition, Tanya spotted the hot pink bow she'd wrapped around the handle on her suitcase, making it stand out from the scattering of red, white and blue suitcases on the ground the bus driver extracted from the luggage bin underneath the bus. She trudged over and grabbed the handle, rolling it along the ground to her car. She looked up and there was Daniel, a big bouquet of red roses in his arms. "Hi beautiful." He walked up to her, bent to kiss her, a passionate kiss, lasting longer than her tired body wanted to participate in. But she let him kiss her, take her hand, and escort her to his red Camero.

"Hi, babe. Where's *my* car?"

"I'm having it detailed. I wanted to surprise you. How was Phoenix?"

"Exhausting. I'm so tired I feel like I could fall asleep standing even though I napped most of the way."

"Being an athlete is a hard job. Especially, all the things you gymnasts do. All the apparatuses you perform on. The different tricks. I don't know how you ladies do it."

She whipped her head around. Who was this guy and where did her boyfriend, the one that always nagged on her to keep her weight down and had never recognized how hard it was to be a gymnast, go? She perked with a slight smile. "Thanks, Daniel for saying that. It *is* hard."

"I've watched you. You're amazing. So strong and flexible.

"You were there to watch?"

"By the time I worked through the crowd after the meet you'd gotten on the bus, and it rolled away before I could see you. I waved but you must not have seen me. So, I headed home."

"Oh, that's too bad. I wished I could have talked to you. Give you a hug and a kiss at least."

"Bad timing I guess." He shrugged. "Let me take you back to my place. I'll draw a hot bath for you while I set the table and get dinner ready."

This was why she was with Daniel. He could be so caring and thoughtful. She didn't know why she had thought about Nash so much on the bus ride home, but she was going to enjoy Daniel taking care of her. "That's sounds wonderful. Can't wait."

They reached his car and took off for the thirty-minute drive to his apartment. They had shared an apartment several months ago, but the coaches insisted that the athletes live together within each sport, so she'd moved in with a couple other gymnasts, closer to the gym for practices.

Tanya looked out the window at the Rockies on the horizon and felt glad to be back home. Seemed every muscle in her body ached. It had been a long competition circuit. Colorado Springs and Denver at the universities, Salt Lake City, and then Phoenix all within ten days, and now she was finally home. She reached across the console and held Daniel's hand.

"You have a few days off now, don't you?"

"Yeah, four days. Coach wants us to rest a little bit, but not too much. He wants us to stretch every day, of course."

"I have a surprise for you."

"More surprises? You're spoiling me."

Daniel smiled his perfect white smile. "I like spoiling you."

"What is it?"

He smirked. "Look in the glove compartment."

Tanya snapped open the panel. She pulled out an envelope, peeked inside and took out a plane ticket. "A ticket to Davenport." She leaned over and kissed Daniel on the cheek. "I've missed Miranda so much. I haven't seen her in a month. And I miss that baby too." She reached over and squeezed his hand. "How'd you know?"

"I figured you could use a Graaf shot of farm and horses."

"You're the best, Daniel." Her eyes filled. "Thank you. Thank you."

Daniel drove his Camero into the parking lot of his apartment complex and parked. "Let's go, babe, pampering awaits."

As they climbed the stairs to his apartment a thread of mystery, a subtle sinking feeling slithered its way through her belly. Daniel was being so nice, so attentive. She remembered when he was caring, once before when she had a cold and he had chicken soup delivered when he was knee deep in a track competition. Then a month later they had an argument about her weight at an Asian restaurant. But later they smoothed it out and kept going. And then that time when she had a fight with Miranda, and he talked to Tanya afterwards and set her mind straight and she switched her thoughts over to focusing on the Olympics and training. No distractions they'd said then. He was attentive then and let her cry on his shoulder all the way home on the plane. But weeks later there were jabs about weight and arguments about Miranda and how she was bringing Tanya down. Would this end up the same way, where they argued over something after his special attention to her?

But wasn't that what every couple did? Argue and disagree at times? It was healthy for couples to air things out and that made them closer. Didn't it? Tanya flexed her calloused hand on her jeans and decided to put those thoughts aside for now and take advantage of another good time with Daniel. *Don't be so ungrateful,* she thought. *Enjoy this. He's going out of his way to be nice to you. Be thankful,* she told herself. When they entered his apartment, Tanya followed Daniel into the bathroom, and he started a hot bubble bath.

He kissed her. "Enjoy babe. I'm going to make dinner."

Tanya undressed for her bath, eager to start their relaxing evening.

CHAPTER THIRTY-FOUR

Tanya sat in the window seat on the short flight from Colorado Springs to Davenport, Iowa. She looked at the fields as they flew over Nebraska and thought about how even though the Rockies were gorgeous, the flatlands of the central plains gave her a peaceful homey feel deep inside. She was born and raised in the Heartland of the Midwest and the serene imagery and seeing what comes next as you traveled by car or horse gave her security. No mountains or forests in the way. Right then, she needed that. Her nerves were through the roof and the thoughts about Daniel and fantasies she'd been having about Nash unnerved her. She needed a farm fix and her bestie, Miranda, to set her straight and get her on the right path forward. Miranda and Justine were her home base and even though they weren't her family, they felt like it to her.

Less than three hours later, her plane had landed, and they were on the ground and Tanya stood, grabbing her overnight bag from the overhead compartment waiting while the line of people exited the plane. Tanya scurried through the crowd once she was inside the terminal. She spotted Miranda at the boarding gate and rolled her bag toward her. They hugged each other tightly. It had only been a month but felt longer. "Ran, I missed you so much," Tanya said. They started walking toward the doors leading to the parking lot. "Where's Emily?"

"Mom's spoiling her. She'll take any chance she gets to be a grandma. So, when she offered to watch her while I picked you up, I accepted. I love my daughter more than anything but it's nice to have a few minutes peace now and again." Miranda chuckled. "Who knew babies could be so needy?"

"Give me a break." Tanya nudged Miranda's arm. "You love being a mom."

Miranda beamed. "I know."

They walked arm and arm swiftly through the airport doors and out into the parking lot, headed for Miranda's truck. Tanya threw her overnight bag in the truck bed and got in. She gestured toward the car seat in the middle of the truck bench. "It's so weird seeing you with baby stuff."

Miranda reversed out of the parking spot and drove along the road toward the exit leading to the freeway.

"It fits you though. I always knew you'd be a mom. You're such a caring person."

Miranda took the ramp to the freeway and once they were headed toward Dewitt she glanced over at Tanya. "I could see you being a mom too."

"What? That's the furthest from my mind."

"You find the right guy, and it'll happen."

"Maybe I've found the right guy with Daniel."

Miranda didn't say anything, looked straight ahead and kept driving. On the side of the freeway clusters of silver maple and wire mesh fencing lined the fields next to the road.

"Ran?"

She kept driving.

"You don't like him, do you?"

Finally, Miranda glanced at Tanya then back at the freeway. "It's not up to me who you're with. You know, Daniel called me and asked about you coming to visit. I thought it was really sweet that he wanted to surprise you with a trip home."

Tanya smiled. "He's been attentive lately. He picked me up after my competition circuit and he had roses and brought me back to his apartment. I was so tired. He drew a bath for me and gave me a massage. He even made my favorite dinner."

"Wow. Sounds nice. I miss having a man around."

"Sorry. I don't mean to rub it in."

"I'm happy for you. If you're happy, I'm happy with who you spend time with. Ya know, Daniel also asked if Nash was going to be around. Just so happens Nash is at a rodeo this weekend. He calls me regularly to check up on me. I know it's Hank asking him to do that."

Tanya's face reddened as the heat rose from her belly up to the top of her head. She couldn't believe Daniel was still holding on to when she helped out at the farm when Miranda was pregnant.

"Tanya. What's wrong?"

"I can't believe he doesn't trust me." Tanya looked over at Miranda. "Why are you smiling?"

"I've seen how you look at Nash. You like him."

"He's hot but that doesn't mean I *like* him, like him."

"You *like* him, like him." Miranda guffawed. "Couple days after I brought Emily home from the hospital, I saw you both out in the pasture getting Red. You guys were really close, only a few inches apart. And it seemed like he likes you too."

Tanya sliced her hand through the air. "We were just taking care of Red. We happened to be on either side of his head. That's all."

Miranda turned off the exit heading toward the town of Dewitt. "Then why is your face flushed, Tonny?"

"Stop it. I'm with Daniel. He's the one for me." Tanya wasn't quite ready to talk about the feelings and confusion she'd had over the two guys, even to Miranda. She flipped her ponytail through her fingers. "Daniel and I have more in common. It'd never work with the cowboy. Two different lives." Tanya stared out the window as the truck bumped along the gravel road that led to the Graaf farm. Tanya couldn't tell even her best friend the feelings she had for Nash. It was just a passing crush was all. It'd end soon enough, and she could focus solely on Daniel. Her guy. Stress did this to a person. She was under a lot of pressure to win the gold. Of course she would have a fantasy. It was a diversion to keep her sane through all the training and intensity of competition. Daniel was her reality. Besides, no relationship was perfect. And neither was theirs. But it was right for them. Two elite athletes striving to win gold at the Olympics. They were a team.

As Miranda turned into the driveway of the Graaf farm, she said, "Whatever you say, Tonny. I just want you to be happy."

When they got out of the truck, Ben came running and barking from behind the barn. He ran up to Tanya and jumped up on her. "Hi, buddy, she said." He licked her face. She laughed. "It's good to see you too."

Miranda said, "You *are* part of the family. He missed you."

Justine came out of her house and onto the back porch. She had a baby monitor in her hand. She walked down the steps, tucked the monitor in her back pocket and gave Tanya a hug. "How's our star?"

"Hi Mrs. Graaf. Good. I missed you guys."

"I made some cookies. They're still warm, on the cooling rack."

Tanya patted her belly. "Only one." She smiled. "I'll savor my one and only cookie later, after I settle in at Miranda's. When I'm done with the Olympics, I'm going to let it all go and eat what I want. I don't care if I gain fifty pounds then. Because I won't have to carry my body in the air."

Justine asked, "What will you do afterwards? Have you thought about that at all?"

Tanya shrugged.

"You're probably too focused." She squeezed Tanya's arm. "You'll figure it out. You're a smart girl."

Emily's voice echoed in Justine's back pocket. "Emily is awake. She had a long nap. Good timing, you two."

Miranda said, "I'll go get her." Justine handed her the monitor and Miranda headed for the back door.

Tanya examined Justine's face. "You look amazing, Mrs. Graaf, lighter somehow. What's going on in *your* life?

Justine locked arms with Tanya as they strode toward Miranda's house. "I'm teaching kindergarteners another year in the fall, planting my garden and enjoying living the farm life." She chuckled. "Oh. And Richard and I broke up."

Tanya stopped and looked at her. "Are we happy about this?"

"It was for the best. It was sad to see him go. But there were too many differences."

"Well, you look great. Don't take this the wrong way, but I never thought he was the right guy for you. Too controlling. He wouldn't let you be yourself. You seem happier now."

Justine laughed. "Don't beat around the bush, Tanya. But I am happier now. I can do what I want without someone questioning things I love, like seeing my granddaughter grow up and living on the farm, a place I've always loved. I didn't know how much, until Richard tested me with his wanting me to move to Chicago." She nudged Tanya with her shoulder. "Enough about me. Tell me all about you. Sounds grueling when Miranda told me about riding the bus to different competitions all over the west."

They continued walking toward Miranda and Hank's house at the back of the property. "It was." She sighed. "The life of an athlete." Tanya's focus veered off to the barn. "Who's that?"

Justine glanced over. "That's Dr. De Van. He's a vet over in Clinton."

"What's he doing here?"

"Miranda and he are working on a horse project together. He's a researcher and Miranda is helping him collect data. She's volunteered her horses in the project."

Tanya noticed Miranda heading toward Dr. De Van. She was pushing Emily in a stroller. He smiled and gestured toward the barn. When Miranda reached his truck, she motioned to the barn, they both looked at the same time and laughed.

It was like they had a private joke between them, just like couples do. What was Miranda doing with this tall, blond titan? The two hugged and he left in his dually and nodded as he passed Justine and Tanya. Hmm, thought Tanya, she'd have to talk to Miranda later. What was Miranda playing with? Fire?

After Dr. De Van left, Miranda joined them, and they all strolled to her house.

Tanya said, "What were you and the doc laughing about?"

Miranda hesitated and nervously gave a smile. "Ben and Petey. They were in the barn when Gerrit was examining one of the horses. He offered to take Petey back to the Browns' next door."

"Wait. What? Isn't that what Hank used to do? Take Petey back to the Browns'?"

Miranda's face flushed like she got caught with her hand in the cookie jar.

Tanya would *definitely* have that conversation with Miranda later about the titan.

CHAPTER THIRTY-FIVE

The next day, Miranda and Tanya woke up after hours of girl talk the night before, catching up about the month they'd been apart. Miranda had mostly talked about what it was like being a mother. Tanya mostly talked about what competing, living and breathing gymnastics was like as the time got closer and closer to the Seoul Olympics.

They padded into the living room, Tanya carrying mugs of coffee. Miranda settled on the couch as she held Emily to her chest and patted her back. Tanya took a chair nearby and put Miranda's mug on the coffee table.

They continued their conversation from the previous night, both treading lightly when it came to speaking of Gerrit or Nash. Tanya commented on how Daniel excelled in hurdling and the relay. He was the best sprinter on the U.S. team.

Miranda shared how hard it was to have Hank in jail. She talked at great length about her sad, mad, and confused feelings as to why he would lie by omission.

Tanya tried to convince her friend to hang in there. She said, "Knowing Hank, he'll do more than anything to make it up to you, Ran. He's a good man. He'll do right by you." She shifted on her chair and sat crossed-legged. Her eyes gazed softly as she empathized. "You'll have to figure out a way to forgive him."

Miranda said, "I don't know if I can. At least I'm not ready to forgive him *yet*. His going to jail really hurt me and our family. I am so angry." She looked at the bundle in her lap. "I have all I can do to take care of Emily and keep my practice going."

"I'm here for you when I can. Once these Olympics are over, I'll be here as much as you need me."

"That's not until the fall. Hopefully, Hank will be home by then." Miranda's shoulders sank a little and she gently caressed one of Emily's tiny hands. "It seems like so long from now. The last time we visited he looked so sad and thin. He looked like he hadn't eaten. It gets to me. I can't do anything for him. He can't do anything for us. Being in jail is so hard on the family."

Tanya stretched her legs out, pointed her toes onto the coffee table, and laid her chest in a forward bend onto her thighs. "It is, Ran. You're strong. You'll make it through. He'll make it through."

Miranda put Emily to her chest and thumped lightly on her back, not saying anything, staring off into space.

Tanya's eyes bulged as she spotted a dually and horse trailer coming down the driveway and parking in front of the barn. "I thought he wasn't going to be here."

"Who?" Miranda cradled Emily and walked to the window looking outside. "Nash *did* come." She smirked. "He told me he was going to be at a rodeo this weekend." She glanced at Tanya whose mouth was wide open. Miranda said, "That's what I told Daniel when he called about your plane ticket."

Miranda turned back to the window. "I wonder who he brought with him?" She noticed a tall, lean, older gentleman, about her mom's age, wearing a cowboy hat and boots, getting out of the passenger side of the rig. Miranda headed for the door and put her hand on the door handle.

"Where are you going?"

"Outside to say hi. They're here for a reason or they wouldn't have come all the way from Wyoming. It's not like they're just passing by. Come on Tonny." Miranda gave her a smug look. "Don't be bashful."

"What about…"

"What?"

"You know, Daniel. He's going to be mad if he finds out Nash was here. Not that there is anything between us. It's just that Daniel is sensitive to other guys around me."

"That's one way to look at it," Miranda said under her breath.

Tanya frowned. "What'd you say?"

"Oh, nothing. Come on Tonny. Come with me so I don't have to deal with these guys alone." Miranda knew her real reason was to get Nash and Tanya together. Maybe if her friend saw Nash more often, Tanya would realize who the better choice in guys was. She could finally see her bestie with someone that could make her happy. And Miranda knew that someone was not Daniel.

Just as Miranda was walking toward the guys by the rig, Justine came out of her house and strode to them. She raised her hand. "Hello, Nash. Hi Walt."

Miranda wondered, how her mom knew the guy? Who was he anyway?

Walt reached over to shake Justine's hand. "Howdy, Ma'am. Nice to see you again."

Miranda looked back and forth from this man to her mom. What was going on?

"Miranda, this is Walt, Nash's boss from Wyoming. Walt, this is Miranda."

They shook hands. Walt said, "Nice to meet you."

"You're Hank's old boss?"

"I am. Shame what happened. He didn't deserve it."

Miranda tilted her head slightly downward. "Thanks."

Nash said, fighting a smile, "Hi, Tanya. Nice surprise. Didn't know you'd be here."

She blushed. "Nice to see you. Miranda told me you were at a rodeo."

"Change of plans. We were in Cedar Rapids at a show scouting horses. It's only an hour from here so we wanted to come and see if you needed anything."

"That's nice of you." Miranda cocked her head. "Hank put you up to this?"

"He is concerned about you, yes. We wanted to come anyway."

Justine perked and clasped her hands together. "Why don't you stay for dinner? I've got lasagna in the freezer. I can put it in the oven. The least we can do for the trip out of the way."

Walt tipped his hat. "Very kind of you, Justine."

Miranda heard thumping inside the trailer behind the dually. She said, "If you want let the horses out in the pasture or barn while you're here."

Nash went to the back of the rig and opened the door. He hooked a lead rope to one of the horses and began leading the first of four horses, one by one off the trailer.

Tanya stepped up to the trailer. "I can help."

Miranda knew her friend had feelings for that cowboy. She just needed to come to her senses and get rid of that track star.

CHAPTER THIRTY-SIX

Nash smiled at Tanya, the tip of his cowboy hat hiding his forehead, and in the shadow, his clear gray eyes, sent a sizzle of energy and a trickle of excitement throughout her body.

His stare fixed straight at her eyes, and he hesitated slightly for only a moment, then he said, "Thanks." He handed her the rope. "One of the empty stalls for now."

As Tanya grasped the lead, Nash's hand brushed her finger. She blushed and started walking, leading the chestnut toward the barn. And here she was. Again. What was wrong with her? She was with Daniel. Over and over in her mind she repeated this to herself. Why couldn't she get that clear. It was her body's fault. Her mind was trying its best. But it was the sensations she felt whenever she thought of Nash. When she was next to him, her body didn't listen to her mind at all.

After latching the new horse into the stall and heading outside to get another horse, Nash came into the barn, leading a palomino. When Nash stopped in front of Tanya the horse thrust his head up and down and pawed the cement floor. She could empathize with this horse. She wanted to paw the floor and throw her head in the air and scream. Or wrap her arms around Nash and lead him to the stacks of straw in the back of the barn.

She could only imagine what might happen then. But she knew she'd partly lost her mind and if they took it to the straw, she'd be completely gone. All bets would be off then.

She gathered her wits, lassoing her thoughts, and said, "Pretty horse. I've always loved palominos. Beautiful gold and white." She reached to stroke the horse's face.

"All of the horses in the trailer are Quarter Horses. Walt wants to breed them. One of the reasons we went to that show."

Nash's deep voice started loosening the rope around her thoughts.

"It's good to see you, Tanya."

"Good to see you, too." The vision of him in Phoenix flashed across her mind. "Were you at my competition?"

Nash smiled. "Didn't think you saw me."

"I saw you and then when I finished my routine and looked up, you were gone. I doubted you were there, that I *actually saw* you."

"I was there and watched you on the beam and the big mat doing flips and dancing."

She looked at him waiting for him to finish, her lips slowly forming a smile.

"You were so amazing to watch. I can't get over how you can do all that stuff." Nash shook his head slowly. "A bull rider has nothing on you. The strength…"

Tanya wanted to do more, a lot more, but reached for his hand and squeezed it. "Thank you, Nash. I appreciate you coming all that way to watch me. It means a lot."

"I've wanted to tell you…I can't seem to stop thinking about…"

Just then, Walt came into the barn leading another chestnut. He tipped his cowboy hat. "Sorry for interrupting." He had a smirk on his face.

Tanya wondered if Walt knew what Nash was thinking, but she was relieved that he had interrupted what Nash was about to say, and yet there was a part of her, a big part if she was honest with herself, that wanted to hear him out. Whenever they were together, the spark between them ignited and burst like a finale of fireworks at a Fourth of July party. Was she creating things or did Nash feel what she did or was it all in her imagination?

It seemed like the more she tried to pack away her feelings for Nash, put them inside a compartment within her mind like a duffle bag with all her gymnastics gear, the harder it was to keep those feelings of attraction for Nash secured. She was so disciplined when it came to training and gymnastics. She was even strict when it came to eating the right things and not going off the rails, eating a dozen cookies which she wanted to do every day. Or a whole cake or pie. She was able to keep those feelings of desire packed away and not let them take a hold of her sensibility and run wild. But when it came to corralling her feelings for Nash, it seemed she had no willpower. They were too strong.

In every area of her life she had strength, willpower, and common sense about what she needed, but with Nash it was like flailing high into the air doing flips and turns and handsprings, getting caught by what gymnasts call a "twistie": not knowing where she was or how to land. She felt out of control, and nothing seemed to be able to stop her strong feelings of attraction, galloping towards her like a wild horse at full speed. The thrill and fear of what she felt scared her.

What was she going to do? What could she do? The more she tried to reel herself in with common sense the more she felt out of control. Tanya reached for the Palomino's lead rope, took it from Nash and headed for a nearby stall.

CHAPTER THIRTY-SEVEN

It had been a long time since Justine had the pleasure of enjoying cooking a meal for a group of people. Since Richard and she broke up, she had been preparing dinner for one which she found uninspiring. She'd been making a lot of sandwiches for herself lately so it thrilled her she could put together a real meal for the cowboys, Tanya, and Miranda.

An hour later, they all gathered around Justine's kitchen table. The baby was upstairs sleeping, Justine sitting between Miranda and Tanya. Walt and Nash sat opposite them, in a circle around the large round table. Ben scratched at the door. Miranda looked at her mom.

Justine said, "Ben feels left out. Go ahead and let him in.

Miranda opened the back door. "Come on, buddy." Ben padded into the kitchen; his nose tipped upward at the food: lasagna, garlic bread, corn from the freezer and salad from the greens in her garden. The dog circled to Nash and Walt where he sniffed Walt's legs and then he laid right next to Walt on the floor.

Miranda smiled. "He's taken to you, Walt."

Justine noted how when Richard was with her, Ben never took a liking to the man no matter how much he tried. Ben must have known he wasn't good for Justine.

They filled their plates and started eating. Walt said, "This is nice of you to go out of your way. Been a long time since I ate a home cooked meal like this."

Walt was tan with a sun weathered face, lean and strong build, maybe six foot tall. His light blue eyes sparkled as if he had a story to tell. His calloused hands picked up the salad bowl and he scooped some greens onto his plate. Something about him reminded Justine of Stanley. Maybe farmers and ranchers had similar qualities. Good work ethic. Respect for the land and adapting to rhythms of nature. Long hours outside and mental and physical endurance. Stanley had had that same salt of the earth quality.

Justine said, "Everything is from our farm."

Walt smiled. "There's nothing like home grown food." And he took a bite of garlic bread.

"It's a pleasure to cook for someone who appreciates farm food. Please, help yourselves to more."

Walt and Nash each scooped seconds of large servings of lasagna and corn on their plates.

Nash said, "Real tasty, Ma'am."

"You gentleman and your ma'am's." She gave a dismissive wave of her hand. "It makes me feel old. Please call me Justine."

Tanya shot nervous glances at Nash. He'd wanted to tell her something in the barn. Something about when he was in Phoenix watching her in the gymnastics meet. Why had he gone there in the first place? It frustrated her that she had to wait until later to find out. She felt too anxious to eat. Tanya picked at her lasagna, taking a tiny bite and then a small forkful of corn. Garlic bread with butter was off her diet until after the Olympics.

Justine announced, "Save room for dessert. I made a banana cream pie."

Walt grabbed his belly. "You're spoiling this cowboy. I won't be able to walk for a week."

After dessert, Miranda trotted upstairs to check on Emily. She came back downstairs and said, "I need to get back to work. Can you call me on the office phone when she wakes up, Mom?"

"I will, honey. Don't work too hard."

Miranda headed for the clinic.

Nash glanced at Tanya, and they locked eyes. Tanya said, "Thank you for dinner, Justine. I'm going to check on the horses. Maybe look at what the guys bought at the show."

"Thanks, Justine." Nash rose. "Better get to it."

Walt glanced at Justine, his brow raised slightly, and she responded with a tiny smile.

Nash followed Tanya across the back yard and caught up to her when she entered the barn.

Tanya turned to look at him. He almost ran into her. They were barely a few inches apart. She croaked, "What did you want to tell me before?"

"Before?"

"Don't play dumb. You know exactly what I'm talking about. Before Walt came into the barn with some horses. Seemed like you wanted to give me a reason why you came to watch me in Phoenix." She put her hands on her hips. "Why *did* you come to watch me, Nash?"

He looked at her, deep into her soul with those clear gray eyes, deep pools of sky, full of storm and rain. Tanya longed to jump into his arms and have him hold her, blend together like two peas in a pod. Salt and pepper. Horse and rider.

After a long pause, that filled her belly with swirls of falling snow, melting on a hot engine, Nash's deep voice sounded like music from a cello, rich and warm. "I can't seem to stay away from you."

Tanya's face grew hot. She felt the same way. This crazy feeling she had when she was around Nash or even thought about him. Her lips grew into a slow smile. They stood there at the entrance to the barn and looked at each other, close.

Heat rose within the two inches between them like steam escaping from a tea kettle. Tanya didn't want to move. She wanted to kiss Nash. But she couldn't. She didn't want to be a cheater. She was faithful to whomever she was with. The temptation was so strong, the two inches shortened to one inch, and then a horse kicked his stall and screeched, startling them.

Nash jerked away from Tanya. "I'd better go see what's up."

At the main house, Walt and Justine sat on the porch. Justine brought out fresh coffee on a tray and they settled in. It was a sunny day, late in spring and sixty degrees. They enjoyed the warmth coming from the afternoon sun.

As Justine chatted with Walt about the weather and growing crops, she had flashbacks of sitting on the porch with Stanley a few years prior and how similar the two men were. They both respected the outdoors and weren't afraid of hard work. They both worked with animals and knew how to take care of their homes. One, a ranch, the other, a farm. One wore cowboy hats, the other, John Deere baseball caps.

And then more recently the time she had spent with Richard and the close call that she almost married him. A month after she'd last seen him, she had the distance to realize it would have been a huge mistake to spend the rest of her life with Richard. And she would have given it her all, and even though they may not have blended together very well, she would have stayed married to him. Because that was who she was, someone who made good on her promises.

The desire for connection and warmth clashed with her loyalty to Stanley. She realized now that she'd gotten involved with someone else too soon when she'd dated Richard. She had committed herself to her husband, and being with another man contradicted her promise to Stanley. Although the commitment was intended to last until death, she continued to love Stanley and maintained her loyalty to him.

As she talked with Walt, Justine asked herself, could she be with anyone else ever again? Let alone marry someone and devote her life to them? She didn't know. But this man sitting next to her touched something deep down that she'd felt long ago. It scared her.

Maybe Walt sensed her fear because he understood. "Thank you, Justine, for the good food and conversation. Haven't had an afternoon like that in a long time. Reminds me that I need to slow down and take in the moments, ya know?"

"I do. Time goes so quickly, the older I get."

Walt tipped his hat. "I'll go see what Nash is up to. We need to get back."

Words took over and fell out of Justine's mouth before she could stop them. "You're welcome any time. Stop by next time you come to Iowa." She couldn't believe she said all that. The last thing she wanted to do was get into a relationship. Her life was full as it was. But she could always use another friend.

Walt smiled a big smile that made her blush. "I'd love that." He turned and walked away.

Justine watched him as he headed to the barn. Yes. She could always welcome more friends in her life.

CHAPTER THIRTY-EIGHT

It was the middle of June and Justine felt like having a party. Vegetables were growing in her garden, the grass was green, and the weather was warm and Justine's favorite time of year. The corn had been planted in the fields by the Brown's and was about ankle high.

After Stanley died, Justine had hired help to do the harvesting of the corn and soybeans. This year it was corn, and she hired the Van Burens' son for the job. Jake began helping his dad when he was a teenager and now, he and his wife and baby lived in a house they built on the Van Buren property. Jake had taken over the huge farm the year before and his father, Mr. Van Buren, helped his son now. Their farm had been in the family four generations much like the Graaf farm.

For her party, Justine invited the Van Burens, Stanley's nephew, Larry, and his wife and three kids, and of course Miranda and Emily.

She invited the Browns, but Mrs. Brown sounded awkward and hesitant, saying they couldn't make it, not giving any particular reason. In fact, Justine hadn't spoken to the Browns in a couple months, about the time Hank went to jail. She hoped everything was ok with them.

Pastor Bob was bringing his new wife, Susan. Justine was excited to meet her.

Justine went out to her garden in the morning to pick some lettuce, cucumbers, spinach and radishes for a salad. Then she filled a basket with green peppers, kohlrabi, and carrots for dipping.

She marinated several pieces of chicken for barbecuing on the grill, formed some hamburger patties, and checked to make sure she'd bought enough hot dogs from the butcher in town for the kids. Then she got to work peeling potatoes for potato salad.

Mid-morning, Miranda tapped on the kitchen door and then came in. "Hi, Mom. Big day today. Can I help?"

Justine glanced over her shoulder as she continued working at the sink, flicking off potato skins from the large Idahos she'd purchased the day before at Hy-Vee. Her potatoes wouldn't be ready for at least another month, maybe two, depending on the weather. "Thank you, honey. But you have enough to do with the horses." She turned her body to face Miranda, potato and peeler still in her hand. "Where's Emily?"

"Stephanie is watching her at the house."

"She's been a big help for you. You and Dr. De Van 'bout done with your research project?"

Miranda shrugged. "He's trailering a couple horses today from his clinic so we can take a look at their feet. He's teaching me about Equine Laminitis. It's difficult to diagnose and treat."

Justine looked at Miranda, trying to understand the medical terms she was using. "Laminitis? Sounds important. What is that?"

"Sorry. Lately I've been talking a lot to Gerrit using vet terminology. It concerns horses' feet. The new research is saying it may be connected to insulin resistance which is blood sugar metabolism."

"Like diabetes?"

"Mmhmm." Miranda smiled. "Gerrit told me his lab equipment is down - he's waiting for new equipment - but I think he's just being kind, so I don't have to travel with Emily."

Red flags swiped across Justine's mind like the starter at a horse race. She hoped Miranda was being cautious working so closely with the vet. Maybe she could go out to the barn later and peek at what they were doing. "Just be careful," was all she said.

Miranda's forehead scrunched. "I've always been careful around horses' hooves."

Justine lifted one eyebrow. "That's not what I'm referring to."

"Mom? Really. We're professionals." Miranda shook her head and turned on her socking feet and headed for the door. While she picked up her boots and shoved them on her feet, she glanced over and asked. "What time is dinner?"

"Barbecue at five."

"Let me know if you need anything. I'll come early to help you set up."

"Thanks, dear."

Miranda tromped to her house. She remembered the day she returned from her internship in England. A cascade of warmth filled her heart as she recalled the feeling of being in Hank's arms after months away. They had stood holding each other tightly in the driveway and wept they'd missed each other so much. Hank had then taken her hand and shown her with such pride the new house he'd built for them while she was gone.

Did her mom really think that Miranda could easily fall for someone other than Hank? Gerrit was just a colleague. There was no love interest between them. She missed Hank and couldn't wait until he came home. Only a month to go. Her mom didn't know what she was talking about.

She stepped through the front door of her house. Stephanie and Emily were on a blanket on the floor. Stephanie dangled a plastic toy key ring above Emily and they both were smiling. Emily let out a giggle while Stephanie said, "You're a cutey pie. Yes, you are."

Miranda said, "You're not only good with animals you're great with babies too. Is there nothing you can't do?" She smiled.

Stephanie looked up. Her hair was especially poofy today with her brown locks teased on top of her head. She wore a sweatshirt with shoulder pads and bright pink lipstick. "Hi Miranda." She gestured toward Emily. "She's been so good. Wide awake while you were gone. We've been playing the whole time."

"Why don't I feed her and put her down for a nap in my office? You can take the two dogs I have in my clinic for a walk."

Stephanie's lips formed a straight line, and she subtly crossed her arms.

Miranda scooped up Emily and sat on the couch. She patted the cushion next to her. "Come have a seat, Steph." She situated Emily across her lap and began nursing her. "Tell me what's going on with you. It seems like you've only wanted to help the cats I've had in my care the last month."

In the kitchen, the dishwasher hummed and rattled. Finally, after a few moments, Stephanie said, timidly, "I'm afraid of dogs."

"Is this about when you were bitten?"

Stephanie slowly nodded. "I don't know if I'm cut out to be a vet anymore. Or even a vet assistant."

Miranda thought for a moment. "It's ok to be scared, Stephanie. Once my family doctor told me she had a fear of blood even while she was in med school. She would faint at the sight of it. She knew that that wouldn't work if she was going to be a doctor. So, she set out to get over her fear, and the way to do that was to face it. She signed up for every opportunity to work at the lab, draw blood, observe during surgeries, assistant in the ER, work with doctors learning how to stitch up cuts. She even watched medical shows and videos about injuries that had a lot of blood in them. At first, she said that she fainted a couple times. But then she pushed through it and toward the end of her schooling she was so used to the sight of blood that she could even eat a sandwich while working in the cadaver lab."

Stephanie perked. "Really?"

"Yeah. My point is that sometimes pushing through our fears is the best way to get over them. In psychology they call that exposure therapy."

Stephanie drew in a slow and deep breath. "I'll do it then. Can you help me?"

"You bet I will." Miranda shifted a sleeping Emily over her shoulder and burped her gently. "Let's go out to the barn. I'll put her down for a nap."

In the barn, Ben ran towards them from the field. He licked Miranda's hand. When his muzzle searched for Emily's hand, she jerked it away.

Miranda said, "He's a good one to start with. Just take slow breaths and see if you can let him sniff you."

Stephanie stood as rigid as an oak tree and breathed in shaky breaths.

"You're doing fine." Miranda crouched and let Ben lick her hand. She said, "Can you pet his head?"

Stephanie reached out a shaking hand and dabbled a couple fingers on the top of Ben's head.

"You're doing great. Let's go inside and you can clean the cat cages and then I need to put on a new dressing for a cocker spaniel who stayed overnight. If you're up to it, you can help."

While Emily napped, Stephanie had cleaned the cages, swept the clinic floor, and was assisting Miranda with changing the dressing on the spaniel.

"You're doing great, Steph."

"It's easier when you're right there."

"In no time you'll be handling dogs like a pro."

Stephanie smiled and Miranda finished wrapping the dog's shoulder where he had run into barbed wire chasing a squirrel. Barbed wire injuries were a common occurrence for vets in the country. Miranda turned to Stephanie. "Feel like picking up Pepper and putting him back in his cage?

Stephanie tentatively lifted the dog from the metal table and transported him to the cage. When she shut the door, she turned around. "Thanks, Miranda. You've been so patient with me. I don't think I'm completely over my fear but having you here has really helped me get to a better place."

"Glad I could help. You coming to the barbecue later?"

"Yeah, my brothers, dad and my mom are too. I hope your mom made her yummy, barbecued chicken. I'm starving." Stephanie gathered her things and then left for home.

CHAPTER THIRTY-NINE

Later in the afternoon, after feeding Emily, Miranda took her baby to Justine's house for a nap. Gerrit showed up with his trailer. He opened the back and Miranda came outside, ready to help him with more research.

"Hi Miranda. Got a couple of new ones here. I'm betting they have Laminitis too. Their feet are bad. An owner dropped them off this morning, wanting help. They're his kids' ponies that he purchased at an auction."

She led one of the Shetlands and Gerrit led the other into the barn. They hooked a lead rope on either side of the ponies halters that latched to the rings on the walls.

"I took x-rays of their front feet and brought the films with me. I haven't had a chance to look yet. But see how Tony the pinto is rocking back on his hind legs like a rocking horse?"

"Like it's painful to stand on all four legs."

Gerrit removed a metal instrument from his vet bag. "This hoof tester will tell us a lot." He applied pressure to the sole, the underside of the foot, and toe, the front part of the hoof on each of Tony's front legs. Tony jerked his foot up when the hoof tester touched his foot.

"He's in pain, for sure."

Gerrit handed over the hoof tester to Miranda. "Try it with Stormy."

Miranda put pressure on the dapple's feet, although he didn't react like Tony did. She checked his hooves. "It's hot. He's got some inflammation going on."

"I'd like to do some blood tests. The latest research says Laminitis could be connected to high insulin and obesity." Owner said appetite is gone and they haven't eaten since yesterday.

"We'll do a glucose on each of them." Miranda reached into her vet bag and pulled out two syringes to draw blood into tubes that contained sodium fluoride to prevent clotting and inhibit glycolysis, which could artificially lower glucose readings. Once blood was drawn from each pony, she went to her lab and started the testing. She placed the vials in the centrifuge to separate the serum from the red blood cells, ensuring that the reading would be more accurate. While the machine whizzed in a circle Miranda stocked her cupboards with bandages, dressings, rubbing alcohol and antiseptic solutions that had been delivered that morning by Fed Ex.

When the centrifuge stopped, Miranda dropped plasma onto test strips and slipped each one into a glucometer to measure glucose levels for each pony.

Before she could read the results, Gerrit stepped into Miranda's office. He held a large manilla envelope. He clipped an x-ray film onto the illuminated screen of a light box in the corner of her office. Gerrit said, as he pointed to an image. "See how Tony's pedal bone is sinking?"

Miranda nodded. "Stormy's x-ray looks ok, but his digital pulse was strong when I palpated his feet. Could be an abscess?" A month ago, Gerrit published an article in the *Journal of Equine Veterinary Science* about the importance of palpating the pulse in the digital arteries, which are located on either side of the fetlock and blood supply to the hoof. A strong pulse may indicate inflammation or restricted blood flow within the hoof, which could indicate laminitis or abscess. In healthy horses the digital pulse should be faint or barely palatable.

Gerrit was one of the front runners in discovery of the connection between feet, inflammation, and insulin in horses.

After they had looked at the blood test results, Gerrit, along with Miranda's input, decided that Tony had laminitis and Stormy did not. Together, they wrote a treatment plan and put the horses on a low carbohydrate diet, eliminating grains and only hay that has been soaked in warm water for an hour prior to feeding to eliminate simple sugars. They would give them anti-inflammatory medicine to cut the pain. Even though Stormy didn't have full blown laminitis, his blood indicated that his sugar was high-normal, so they put him on the same regiment for prevention. Gerrit would take them back to his clinic later that day.

CHAPTER FORTY

Around five o'clock Justine had set up two picnic tables with plastic silverware, plates and cups. She made iced tea and lemonade, and the grill had simmering coals, ready for chicken, burgers and hot dogs.

The Van Burens were the first to arrive, traveling in their farm dually. Mr. and Mrs. Van Buren got out first; she carried a huge tray covered with tin foil. She glided in her tall six-foot frame over to Justine. "These are my peanut butter brownies. I also made some regular brownies for those who don't like peanut butter."

"Thank you, Eva. How thoughtful of you. You can put them right there, next to the chocolate chip cookies."

The rest of the Van Buren clan came forward and Justine greeted Mr. Van Buren, Jake and his wife, Julie carrying their baby, Jennifer. Justine gushed, "What a sweety, only a month older than our Emily."

Jake and Julie smiled. Jake said, "Sleep is like gold at our house."

"I think if you asked Miranda, she'd say the same thing."

Next, Pastor Bob arrived, with his new wife, Susan. A tall thin woman, standing a couple inches above Pastor Bob, with red hair and fair skin. Her wide-brimmed hat shaded her freckled face.

Pastor Bob said, "Hi Justine." He reached out to shake her hand. "So good to see you." He gestured to his wife. "This is Susan. I don't believe you've met yet."

Justine said, "Hi Susan. Welcome. Please pour some lemonade or iced tea for yourself. The meat is ready to go on the grill."

Just then Miranda came up to the group, holding Emily. Gerrit followed close behind. "Hi everyone. Sorry I'm late, Mom. We got busy with the two ponies we were treating. I'm starving. Anything I can do to help?"

Susan piped in, "This must be your husband, Hank." She offered her hand for a shake.

Miranda's face turned red. The only people who knew Hank's secret were Larry and Stephanie, Gerrit, Nash, and Walt as far as she was aware.

Gerrit directed his arm toward Susan, and they shook. "I'm Gerrit De Van."

Susan looked at him, then Miranda, then Justine, squinting beneath her hat as if the evening sun was blinding her eyes. She put her hand to her mouth. "Sorry, I just assumed."

All eyes were on Miranda and the scene in front of them. Mrs. Van Buren chimed in as she scooped a handful of potato chips and put them on her plate. "Where *has* Hank been? We haven't seen him lately. Used to be two, three times a week he'd return Petey from your farm."

Justine quickly interjected, her words falling out of her mouth like a raft drifting swiftly downstream, "Hank has been very busy lately." She gestured. "Dr. De Van is a vet. Gerrit and Miranda have been conducting a research project. Something about diabetes and horses."

Mrs. Van Buren lifted one eyebrow and poured some iced tea, stirring in some sugar with a tall spoon. She took a sip and looked at Miranda over the rim of her bifocals.

Miranda rolled her eyes to the sky and tilted her head. "Right, Mom, something like that."

"Please, everyone help yourselves to hors d'oeuvres and lemonade or iced tea. There's beer in the cooler too."

Lastly, Larry and his wife and three teenagers came. Miranda went to them quickly to get away from Susan and the rest of the group. She didn't know how long Hank's secret would hold. It had been difficult keeping Hank's whereabouts quiet and the ruse about him being busy, so busy that they had to refer farrier clients to another two towns over was wearing thin.

"Hi guys. I'm glad you could all make it. I have to brag on Stephanie. She is shining, helping me out, and a natural with the animals, and doing a great job."

Stephanie beamed.

Larry said, "Thanks, cuz." He leaned in, saying, "She's got a good teacher."

Miranda smiled. "Go join the party. There's plenty of food. You know my mom, and how much she likes to cook."

Friends and neighbors enjoyed the evening at the backyard barbecue. Lots of laughter and talk about farming and good food. The only hitch was the dark cloud of Hank not being there and Mrs. Van Buren and Susan giving Miranda and Gerrit the eagle eye throughout the evening.

CHAPTER FORTY-ONE

It was the beginning of July and Hank was to be released from jail the following week. Emily was three months old, and it was the first time Miranda was about to be away from her baby overnight. Justine had convinced Miranda to go to the annual veterinarian conference in Ames, Iowa, Miranda's alma mater at Iowa State. The last time she'd been there was over a year before when she graduated. Justine and Emily had formed a strong bond so Miranda felt confident that her mom would be fine watching her daughter. But Miranda was still nervous and called her mom whenever she got a chance, stopping at the gas station pay phones on her drive to Aimes, less than three hours away. Even though she'd only had a child for three months it seemed like she had always had Emily, and it felt strange not to have a child attached to her on her travels.

Gerrit's research project regarding laminitis was moving along. The illness was painful in horses and could lead to chronic lameness if not treated. They'd worked closely together for the past couple months. And she wanted to support him when he'd asked her to assist in his presentation, putting everything together, including his power point and organizing his notes.

A few minutes before the lecture, participants entered the conference room. The walls were covered in dusty rose wallpaper, with beige carpet underfoot and fluorescent lighting hummed from the ceilings. At the front, a large whiteboard stood beside a podium. An audiovisual cart held a large television with a VCR placed on a lower shelf for playing tapes of Geritt's presentation. As attendees arrived, they gathered around the coffee and tea table in the back corner, chatting quietly before taking seats at four-person tables.

A few minutes before Gerrit began his talk Miranda went over last-minute details. For a man who seemed so self-assured and confident when she had been with him the previous months, he seemed nervous about presenting to vet students and colleagues already in practice.

Beads of sweat shown on his forehead from the lights above and he kept wiping his brow with a Kleenex. Gerrit stuttered and stumbled over his words. "Do we have enough information? Did you bring the tapes?"

Miranda placed her hand on his forearm and flashed him with a smile. "You'll be great. They're excited to hear what you have to say, Gerrit."

After perusing the notes that she had organized into index cards, a separate color for each section of the presentation, she reviewed them with Gerrit.

He looked at her with those light blue eyes and gave her a quick hug. "Thanks, Miranda. You've been such help. Couldn't have done it without you."

Miranda took a seat at a table with other participants.

Garrit then stood at the podium, held his shoulders back and with a strong steady voice began his seminar as if nothing had ever bothered him the previous moments.

After the hour-long keynote a few of the students came up to Gerrit at the front of the room by the podium. Miranda stood back feeling so much older and removed from the young students. She was a vet and a mother, and it put her in a whole different life cycle. Miranda looked on as a couple women fawned over Gerrit. She couldn't help feeling a little jealous and it bothered her that she felt that way.

Later, Gerrit invited Miranda to dinner with a few colleagues of his. When they took seats at the large table in the restaurant, she once again felt jealous observing a woman veterinarian he'd gone to school with as she sat next to Gerrit the opposite side of Miranda. Every time Miranda tried to join in, this woman, Barbra, would interrupt and take over the conversation. It became apparent that they had a history more than just classmates.

After dinner, Gerrit walked Miranda back to the nearby hotel.

When they walked into the lobby, Gerrit said, "Do you want to join me for drinks at the hotel bar?"

Miranda looked at him, his clear blue eyes carrying quiet confidence and a warmth that was an unmistakable invitation for something more – an amorous glimmer that called for her to step over the line and take the drinks further into the evening, joining him in his room upstairs. The air between them seemed charged, as though they were the only ones in the hotel lobby and time stood still. Miranda could feel her heart pounding in her ears and her neck and face felt flushed. All the amorous feelings she had toward Gerrit, the last couple of months she had worked closely with him, came to a head. She knew if she went with him her life would never be the same. She and Hank were hanging by a thread as it was, and if she made that choice to be with Gerrit she couldn't go back, and it would ruin their marriage.

Gerrit was tall, handsome, charming, and intelligent. Watching him flexing his strong arms while he handled large draft horses was like looking at Michelangelo's sculpture of David coming alive.

Miranda realized the feelings were a projection of an accumulation of her anger, frustration, and emptiness of not having Hank by her side, raising their daughter and living life. She missed Hank terribly and the emptiness she had felt was filled with the attraction she'd had for Gerrit.

She felt the weight of Gerrit's gaze and knew he wanted her. She'd felt it for months. She took a half step back, putting space between them. "I belong to someone else."

He stood not moving and nodded, still with a hopeful look in his eyes.

"I can't, Gerrit. I won't."

He looked at Miranda with eyes that showed disappointment. But she knew it was the right thing to do. "Have a good night." She turned and walked to the elevator to gather her things.

It was tempting to go with Gerrit. But turning him down felt freeing. It was a chance for Miranda to take a strong stand for her beliefs and commitment to Hank, passing over Gerrit's invitation. She needed to commit fully to making her marriage with Hank work.

Miranda stepped onto the elevator and turned to push the button to her room floor. She looked toward the lobby and saw Barbra and a couple of her friends joining Gerrit and the group walked toward the hotel bar.

CHAPTER FORTY-TWO

That same day, Hank waited in the back of the courtroom with his attorney for his probation violation hearing. Thoughts whirled in his mind, mostly about the audacity that he was there once again, sweating it out, awaiting the judge to give him a sentence. Would he add several months to Hank's already three months' probation? He only had a week left and now this happened. The guard who had been a nightmare to deal with found benny pills underneath his cell mattress during a random check. Hank had been at the jail library doing research about the law and helping one of the inmates learn how to read. One, if not the only satisfying thing about being in jail, was helping other guys better themselves. In the last two months, Hank had three guys reading in the library with him who had never been interested in books before.

But now Hank's future was in the judge's hands once again. How could this have happened? He had never gotten drugs from anyone. Someone must have planted them is all he could think of. Someone who had it out for him. He told his attorney that very thing in one of the interview rooms used by attorneys and visitors while they talked to inmates. Lately, Hank had become more positive as he added up the days he had left before he could finally be with his family. But now, what would happen to him? Would Miranda wait for him if he had to stay in jail longer? It wasn't fair to her, their daughter, or him.

When Hank's name was called, he and his lawyer moved to the table reserved for defendants and attorneys. He walked slowly with leg chains and cuffs on his wrists, and he sat down in his orange jumpsuit and looked ahead, waiting for the judge to start asking questions. He hoped this time his attorney would come through unlike at his sentencing hearing three months prior.

The judge said, "Next on our docket, Hank Driscoll." The judge, a man in his fifties, with short black hair and grey temples stated, "You have been found with drugs in your possession in your cell. How do you plead?"

Hank stood and said, "Not guilty, your honor. Those were not mine."

His attorney intervened. "Mr. Driscoll has stated that these drugs were not his. He has never been involved with drugs. He believes they were planted and that he was set up."

"In that case we'll set a date for a trial." The judge leaned closer to the clerk, standing beside him. And then said, "We'll set a date for a trial in six months on November 15."

Hank's heart collapsed into his feet.

"Your honor, might I ask that we expedite his trial date as he is due for jail release next week."

"As you can imagine, Mr. Smith, our dockets are quite full. If a cancellation should come up, we'll consider moving his date up. In the meantime, November 15 is his scheduled date for a trial." Hank sunk his face in his hands. He didn't know if he'd be able to stand five more months in jail.

The last three months had been a nightmare: Living in a state of hypervigilance, always watching his back, for fear of being attacked in the shower, in his cell, anywhere. Fluorescent lights never dimmed, and buzzed overhead twenty-four hours a day, erasing any sense of night or morning and making it hard to sleep. The constant noise from inmates yelling, doors clanging, echoing off the cement walls. The putrid air, he didn't know if he'd every rid his nose of sweat, disinfectant, and the metallic tang of rusted bars. He felt like an animal, living in a cage.

He'd always taken freedom for granted. But now it was one of the most valuable things in life, second behind his wife and child. But if he couldn't be with them, what was the point in living?

Hank turned to his attorney, and pleaded, "You've got to do something. I was framed. I know you probably hear lies from a lot of desperate people wanting to get out. But. I. Didn't do it. You've got to believe me. It's killing me being locked up."

His attorney must have taken sympathy because he said, "I believe you, Hank. I don't think you did it. I will investigate and see what I can find."

At that moment an officer came up to them. "Time to go, Driskill."

Hank stood and before he was led out of the room, he turned toward his attorney. "Promise me you'll find something."

His attorney nodded.

And Hank was taken back to his cell.

CHAPTER FORTY-THREE

Miranda called her mom from the hotel, asking her to watch Emily for an extra day. She packed up her things and instead of going home, she drove all night to Cheyenne. In the early morning, she steered her truck into the jail parking lot, parked, and rushed into the building. At the reception desk she asked if she could see Hank Driskill. The man at the desk told her it was not visiting hours yet. She looked him straight in the eye with the most commanding stare and said, "I have driven all night from Iowa. I don't care what visiting hours are." She pounded her fist on the counter. "I want to see my husband."

The man succumbed. "I guess there isn't any harm in it. There isn't much going on right now. Just a minute." He left the room.

Hank had laid in bed, sleepless from his hearing the previous day. His thoughts swirled like a car on an icy road spinning out of control with images of the veterinarian from Clinton, taking Hank's place as a husband, and raising his daughter. Hank lay awake, going over in his mind what had happened and what he was going to do to get out of captivity. He was innocent and he was going to prove it. He looked up when he heard the lock on the door to his cell clanking. A guard said, "Driskill. There's someone to see you."

Thinking it was his attorney, Hank threw his long legs over the side of his bunk, got up, rubbed a hand over his sleep-deprived face and followed the man to the visiting area. When Hank turned the corner into the room a flush of adrenaline shot through him. It was Miranda. Her face looked eager and much more positive than the last time he'd seen her, with Emily. Where was their baby?

Because they couldn't touch, he sat down across from her at the table and reached his hand towards her. "Babe."

The guard said, "No contact."

"I'm so glad to see you. Where's Emily?"

"At home with Mom. I was at a vet conference helping a colleague and I just had to see you."

Hank wanted desperately to know who this "colleague" was. He had suspicions about the vet in Clinton. But he didn't dare ask her about him. Who was he to ask her questions about who she was with and what she was doing?

She looked at him with eager eyes. "I need to tell you something."

The air in his lungs rocketed out of him. Had she fallen in love with the vet from Clinton? Was she leaving Hank?

Miranda looked downward, paused for a moment. Then she said, "I was helping Gerrit, the vet from Clinton. We've been working on a project over the last couple months." She played with her dangly earring.

Acid climbed up his throat and he forced a swallow.

"At the conference, Gerrit asked me out for a drink at the hotel bar. I knew what would happen after that, he'd want me to go to his room." Miranda paused.

"Go on." Hank gripped the side of his chair to steady his churning stomach. His heart sank into a hole so deep he didn't know if he could ever retrieve it back into his chest.

"But I realized in that moment how much I love you and how much I want our marriage. I didn't want to complicate things with us more than they already are. You made a mistake. No one is perfect. We all make mistakes." Miranda had tears in her eyes. "I love you so much. I am all on board making us work. Whatever we need to do. I'm team Hank." She smiled. "I'm team us."

Hank exhaled audibly the breath he'd been holding. His sunken heart flung back into his chest. Tears spilled from his eyes. He knew the guard would see it as a sign of weakness, but he didn't care. Before him was his life, his love and she was with him all the way. What a gift. To have Miranda Graaf as his wife. He would be eternally grateful. "Babe." He swiped tears from his face. "You are my life. You and Emily are everything to me. I've been so afraid you were going to give up on me."

"Never. Babe. Never."

"I have to tell *you* something."

She nodded, her brow furrowed as she urged him forward.

"Someone set me up. I went to a hearing yesterday." Hank told her about the drugs in his possession. "The judge has given me five more months. I've got to get out of here."

"Honey. I'm going to hire a big shooter that can do a good job and find out what is going on. I know you didn't do this. That's not you."

"Thank you, babe."

The guard said, "Times up, Driskill."

Hank rose and looked at Miranda. "I love you more than ever."

She air kissed him. "You and me, babe. We'll get you out of here."

Miranda watched her husband leave the room before she headed for the parking lot. She had a long drive, but despite a night without sleep, she had lots of energy and steered her truck onto the freeway toward home.

After several hours driving on the I-80 freeway Miranda could barely keep her eyes open and took an exit to McDonald's. She was anxious to see Emily and determined more than ever to find a good attorney for Hank, but she knew she needed to take care of herself too. She locked her doors and slept for a couple hours. Upon waking, she bought a large coffee and continued.

When she pulled into the driveway of the Graaf farm, Miranda parked and sat for a moment, taking in the beauty of the night. The stars sparkled like diamonds in the vast velvety indigo blanket of the sky. She breathed in a slow deep breath and exhaled, feeling more hopeful than she had in months.

She jogged up to Justine's back door and was about to knock when Justine peeked her head out and held the door for Miranda. "Hi, honey." She clutched her robe to her chest. "I was getting worried. You drive all night?"

She *tsked*. "You worry too much."

Justine tugged her arm. "Come in."

Thanks, Mom. I appreciate you taking care of Emily. She upstairs?"

"She's been asleep now for about an hour. It was hard to get her to sleep tonight, more so than last night. I think she misses you."

"I'll just go up and give her a kiss."

"I'll make some hot cocoa."

After Miranda checked in on Emily, gazing at her sleeping soundly in the old crib that Miranda had slept in as a baby, she headed downstairs. Justine had a plate of berry muffins on the table. She handed Miranda a mug and gestured to sit down. "How'd the trip go?"

Miranda told her about her visit with Hank and that she was excited about getting him home so they could be a family.

Justine perched at the table listening to her daughter and when Miranda had finished Justine said, "I'm so relieved, honey. For a while I thought you were getting too close to Gerrit and wondered if you'd give up on Hank."

Miranda shook her head. "I love him, Mom. He and Emily are my family, my world. I'm all in. Now I need to find a good lawyer." She put her hand on Justine's. "Thank you for trusting that I'd figure this out on my own. It had to have been hard seeing me flounder. And Mom, you're my family too. You've helped me so much in the past months with Emily. I don't know what I would have done without you supporting me."

"You're welcome, honey. You're a good mom."

Miranda took a muffin and bit into the chewy goodness. "Mmm, raspberries and blueberries. You're also the best cook. Maybe your cooking talents skipped a generation. Emily may be your prodigy when it comes to baking and cooking. Cuz it sure isn't me."

Justine smiled and scooted the plate of muffins toward Miranda. "You've got other things to keep you busy."

"How are you doing, Mom? Without Richard and all? I've been so focused on myself and Emily that I haven't asked about you."

"Ya know, I'm doing just fine. I missed him at first, but then I realized the things that I love most he just couldn't accept. He wanted me to be someone different. I want to live here on the farm. I love my garden and being a teacher and most of all being a mother to you and a grandma to Emily. My life is full."

"You seem lighter somehow. I could see that he was trying to control you but figured it was none of my business."

"Thank *you*, for letting *me* figure things out."

"I just followed your lead. If you're happy, then I'm happy for you."

CHAPTER FORTY-FOUR

Later that week Miranda took Emily with her into downtown Davenport and met with a defense attorney who had won several hard cases. The new attorney, George Bearsley, a balding, stocky man in his fifties, sat at his walnut desk, listening to her story and took notes on a legal pad.

After Miranda finished, he shoved the paperwork aside and took off his readers. He leaned in and straightened his silk tie. "Because I'm only licensed in the state of Iowa, I will need to get "pro hac vice" admission to practice in the state of Wyoming. Since this is an unusual case, and Hank's a resident of Iowa, hopefully the bar will give me permission for this one time."

Miranda held Emily with one hand and the other reached in her purse for her checkbook. She had written a two-thousand-dollar check for a retainer, scraping together the last of their savings.

Mr. Bearsley held up a hand. "You can give my secretary your payment up front at the reception desk."

She perched on the edge of her seat, jiggling Emily on her knee. "I want my husband out of jail within the next month."

"I don't know if that's possible. It can take time to work through the court system."

She looked at him, cocked her head. In a firm, don't mess with me voice, she said, "Do what you gotta do. Just get him out of jail." She rose, turned on her heal, held Emily closely and talked to her as they left the building. "Your daddy's coming home." She looked at her baby and tucked hair away from Emily's face. They tromped to the truck parked on the edge of the sidewalk. Miranda bundled Emily in her car seat, and they traveled back to the farm. Miranda had animals waiting for her in need of care at home.

CHAPTER FORTY-FIVE

The summer Olympics in Seoul, South Korea were September 17 to October 2. It was unusual for the games to be held this late in the season but the climate in Seoul was more conducive to a fall competition because the weather typically tended to be very hot and humid during the summers making it unsuitable for major outdoor sporting events. This decision was made by the International Olympic Committee.

Tanya was ready to compete and disappointed that they had to prolong the competition for a couple months. But the wait was over, and it was time for the performance of her lifetime. This was what all her hard work and sacrifice came down to: stepping onto the Olympic stage, performing the routines she had honed for years—driven by the hope of earning her country's pride.

The United States gymnastics team were arriving a few days earlier to acclimate to the climate and surroundings. Other teams such as the track and field, swimming and volleyball teams, arrived as well. Tanya sat with her teammates on the plane for the 18-hour flight, with one stop in Los Angeles.

Once her gymnastics team was settled in their seats and in the air, Tanya took a pill that her doctor had given her for anxiety for the long flight. She usually didn't like taking medicine because it left her feeling groggy. They were arriving long enough before the competition so she knew it would leave her body and she'd be ready to compete in a few days. She leaned her head back against the headrest hoping to sleep, escaping the last few days of pre-competition jitters that had preceded this flight. It had been a long haul training, competing, and focusing throughout this marathon leading up to the Olympics. All that pressure for a few days of competition.

But that wasn't all that made her exhausted. She ruminated about the week leading up to this trip. Daniel had been acting strangely for the whole month. Tanya chalked it up to the stress of being an elite athlete. They were all under a lot of pressure. But a few nights that she stayed at his apartment instead of her own, he didn't come home. He'd said it was because they trained longer than usual, and he slept on the couch of a buddy that lived next door to the track. He wasn't affectionate and he seemed distant and wasn't even his usual intense self, making sure she ate properly and insistent that she get enough sleep. It was as if he didn't care what she did. He seemed far away and distracted.

One night Daniel asked her out for dinner and insisted that they meet at their favorite Asian restaurant, the place that had a lot of vegetables and healthy food. They had eaten there often over the last several months. It seemed odd he wanted her to meet him there because he would usually pick her up and they'd go together. When she reached the restaurant, he was already sitting at their usual table. Tanya joined him.

He had a serious look on his face. When she sat down, Daniel said, "Tanya, I don't know if you're serious about us. You haven't seemed invested in us."

Tanya started to speak.

He put his hand up. "Let me finish." He glanced downward and then up at her. "I know that you've been seeing Nash."

"What...?"

"I saw him at the competition in Sault Lake City in the spring. And I found out that he was at the farm when you went to visit Miranda."

"I didn't know that he'd be at either of those places." She looked at him. "Are you spying on me?"

"I don't like being lied to or cheated on."

"I haven't done either one of those things. I didn't think it was important to tell you about that." She grimaced. "Why didn't you tell me when you found out? Who told you anyway? You've been acting weird lately. Like you've been staying away from me."

"I had to think about all this." Daniel fiddled with the silverware at his placemat. "I needed to decide what to do moving forward." He looked at her. "I don't think we should see each other anymore."

She shrieked. "You're breaking up with me?"

"You just haven't been as committed as I have been in our relationship. I just think it's best if we both focus on our sports. Not have any distractions. I'll stay with a buddy near the track, and you can have the apartment."

"You haven't been there very much anyway. I'll go back to *my* place." She threw her napkin on the table and marched out of the restaurant. She drove home, tears falling the whole way. When she got back to her apartment she cried some more.

And now two weeks later, she was on the plane to Seoul, sitting next to a teammate when she was supposed to be sitting by Daniel. But he was way up in front of the plane with the rest of the track team.

She closed her eyes and went over her routine for the balance beam, her strongest event, from the mount at the beginning to the end when she dismounted. She visualized flying in a double back flip with a double twist, her most difficult move over and over. But the thoughts about Daniel breaking up with her kept interfering with her sound landing.

Eventually the medication began to take effect, and she slept and dreamed of flipping high into the air and into the clouds. She bounced gently from cloud to cloud and then fell out of one of them. She was falling, falling… past the airplane she was riding in, and she waved at Daniel as she passed the window he looked out of and kept falling farther and farther until she almost hit the ground. Before she crashed though, Nash caught her as she fell into his arms. They kissed long and hard, like her life depended on it.

And then Tanya's whole body twitched, and she woke up.

The gymnast sitting next to Tanya said, "You, ok? You were out as soon as we got in the air."

She rubbed her eyes. "Just had a bad dream. How long have I been asleep?"

The gymnast looked at her watch. "Three hours."

"I have to use the restroom. Excuse me, please." Since Tanya was sitting in a window seat she scooted around the two gymnasts and into the aisle. She walked toward the bathroom and noticed Daniel sitting by another member of the track team. A woman. A sprinter on his team. Tanya had seen her before at practice. She was tall and lean with *long* auburn hair and *long* legs.

Her shiny red hair was wrapped around her shoulders as they huddled laughing.

Once Tanya finished in the bathroom she headed toward her seat. On her way, she passed Daniel again. The redhead and Daniel were sharing potato chips out of a small package. Well, wasn't that interesting? She'd never seen Daniel eat any junk food let alone potato chips. And why were they so chummy? How long had Daniel known this sprinter with the long legs and slender body?

Daniel hadn't noticed Tanya on her way to and from the bathroom he was so engrossed with chumming up to this woman. What difference did it make? Tanya and Daniel weren't together any longer. But why did he really break up with her a couple weeks before? Was he involved with this woman and why did Tanya care?

She sat back down in her seat by the window and thought about the men in her life. Her dad controlled her mom by yelling, intimidation, and physical threats. Her brothers controlled their girlfriends by making jokes about their intelligence, looks and dismissing their opinions and ideas. Tanya rarely saw any of her family, except her mom now and then. The men always made fun of Tanya's gymnastics and knew they wouldn't travel to Seoul to see her. Nor would her mom because she was dependent on her dad.

Tanya thought about how Daniel was like the men in her family. Just a different flavor. Her chest tightened when she thought about their last conversation in the restaurant. But she had been questioning their relationship for months so why was it hard for her and so painful? She wondered if she missed Daniel himself, or just the sense of certainty he brought to her life.

They had been together for a year, and their relationship seemed so right on paper. But it never quite flowed. When it came to training and focusing on their athletic careers, it went fine. They understood each other. They both had that determined and winning attitude. Daniel could be controlling but also kept her on track and disciplined with training. He was a man that supported her athletic dreams and that is why she had been attracted to him, because no other man had been so understanding when it came to her sport. But could she get a medal without him?

She shook off those thoughts and leaned back in her seat, imaging accepting the gold medal for the U.S. and for herself. She'd show Daniel, she didn't need *him* to be an Olympian winner.

It was lunch time, and the flight attendant came round with her meal. She ate all of the chicken parmesan, mashed potatoes and even the chocolate cake and got out a

Cosmopolitan magazine to browse through while she felt satisfaction from eating what she wanted and living her own life without Daniel telling her what to do. She didn't need a man; she could do this on her own. She had her gymnastics team as support, and they would get through the next several days together.

CHAPTER FORTY-SIX

During the same time as Tanya's Olympic competition in Seoul, South Korea, Hank awaited trial in Cheyenne, Wyoming. His big-time lawyer from Iowa brought him a suit to wear for the big day. Miranda and Justine shared driving with Emily in a car seat in the middle of Justine's station wagon to attend the trial. Larry and Stephanie took charge of caring for the animals back home in Iowa.

Miranda and Justine planned on staying for as long as it took for Hank's trial. They checked into a hotel in downtown Cheyenne, within walking distance of the courthouse and jail.

The trial for Hank would be going on at the same time as the Olympics in Seoul and Miranda wanted to watch Tanya on TV when she could. Miranda had wanted to wish her bestie good luck before she left the states. As she unpacked at the hotel room, Miranda mulled over the conversation she'd had with Tanya. Several days prior, Tanya had called Miranda, distressed and crying about Daniel breaking up with her. Miranda was secretly relieved, but she felt sad that her friend was upset and right before the biggest competition of her lifetime.

On the phone, Miranda had listened to Tanya and then tried to give her a peptalk. "Maybe it's for the best, Tonny. Now you can focus on your gymnastics and nothing else to distract you. You're the best and in this way, every ounce of energy can go into winning. I believe in you, Tonny."

Between sniffles she'd said, "Thanks, Ran. I knew you'd make me feel better. You're the best friend a girl could have. But why did he have to break up with me just a few days before we leave for Seoul?"

"Bad timing, for sure. But you can turn it around. You're the strongest person I know. You show him. And win."

"Thank, Ran. I'd better go. I have to pack. I don't know if I'll be able to call you when I'm over there. Good luck with Hank's trial. I hope he gets out soon, Ran. You guys deserve to be a family. Finally."

"Go show 'em what you got, Tonny. Win one for the team, girl. Bring home a medal."

And that's what Miranda needed to do for Hank. Show them what he's got and what a good man he was. They'd get him out of jail. All would be well.

CHAPTER FORTY-SEVEN

On the first day of the trial, Justine stayed with Emily while Miranda went to the courthouse. She sat in the row behind Hank and his attorney. Hank wore a dark gray suit. Miranda blushed as he turned to look at her and smiled, slowly, his sea green eyes full of love. She thought about how handsome he looked and how much she wanted to grab hold of him and wrap her arms around him, finally feeling him next to her after all these months. It had been way too long since they had been together. Her body ached for him. They would do whatever it took to get him out of jail. He had done his time. It was time to come home. They wouldn't leave Wyoming without him.

Over the next few minutes, the courtroom filled with people. The jury had been selected, and the trial began.

The prosecutor presented her findings and made a good case for finding the drugs in Hank's pocket. It would be hard to beat her evidence.

But then Hank's defense attorney began his argument. Mr. Bearsley looked straight at the jury and smiled, showing his most charming attribute. It hooked people into listening intently to what he had to say. Miranda shivered in that he was the typical sleezy perception of the big wig attorneys who made a lot of money. But as he kept talking, Miranda thought that that charming presentation would be what they needed to win this case.

Mr. Bearsley presented his case in which the guard, Mr. Johnson sold drugs to inmates on a regular basis and one of the inmates who didn't like Hank, framed him, placing the drugs in his pants pocket while the men were in the shower. A few minutes later the guards conducted a "random" search on the inmates, and the drugs had been found on Hank's person in his pocket.

A low rumble permeated throughout the twelve jurors as they looked at the guard on the stand ready to testify. He looked indignant and uncomfortable as he shifted in his seat.

The judge asked, "Is this true, Mr. Johnson?"

The guard remained silent, his face turning a crimson shade of red.

The judge said, "Mr. Johnson, please answer the question."

"I plead the fifth."

Mr. Bearsley stood in front of officer Johnson as he placed a hand on the edge of the witness box and looked straight at him. He then backed away and glanced over at the jurors. "I understand you want to plead the fifth, Mr. Johnson. But it may not help your case should you continue with this stance." He looked back at Mr. Johnson. "Be aware that we have witnesses stating that you in fact have been supplying inmates with drugs and you were an active participant in framing Mr. Driskill in this incident we are here for today."

The judge asked again, "Mr. Johnson do you wish to change your response to the question of participating in framing Mr. Driskill?"

Mr. Bearsley added, "Maybe if you knew that one of the witnesses is Jimmy Jones, Hank's old roommate who got released just last month it would help you make a different decision about what you want to say."

Mr. Johnson's face looked like he had been in a tanning booth too long as he replied to the question, "I won't say anything else without an attorney."

The judge nodded to Mr. Johnson. "Would it be fair to say that Mr. Driskill had nothing to do with the drug incident?"

Mr. Johnson nodded his head weakly.

"Please answer the question, yes or no."

"Yes," Mr. Johnson said in a barely audible voice. "He did not have anything to do with it."

The judge nodded to the officer in the court room. "Please retain Mr. Johnson." Mr. Johnson was handcuffed and taken from the courtroom.

"As for the charges against Mr. Driskill, all charges are dropped." The judge looked at the jury. "Thank you for your service. You may go about your day." He then looked at Hank. "Mr. Driskill, the court apologizes for the inconvenience. You have served the entirety of your sentence including probation, community service, and time served because you were in jail two extra months. You are free to go."

Miranda let out a short yelp and cupped her mouth with her hand. She lept from the bench behind Hank as he turned toward her and they threw their arms around each other and hugged tightly. He kissed her again and again. They stood with their arms wrapped around each other and wept. Finally, Hank looked at his attorney. "Thank you." He grabbed Mr. Beardsley's hand in a firm shake.

His attorney said, "You're welcome. It's been a long haul. Good luck to the both of you."

Hank took Miranda's hand in his. "Let's get going. We have a lot to make up for."

Miranda asked, "Do you need to get your things?"

"The only thing I want is right here." He grabbed her into a tight hug and kissed her.

They walked hand in hand along the sidewalk to the hotel where Justine waited with Emily. They reached the door of the room and burst through. Justine screeched, "Hank! You're out!"

He beamed. "I want to hold my daughter. Finally." He went to them. Emily was sleeping as Justine stood rocking her from side to side. Hank scooped the baby into his arms. Tears streamed down his face. "I've waited too long for this moment." He stared at her and stroked her face lightly with his finger. "She's so beautiful." His eyes fixed on his daughter for several minutes. He then turned to Miranda. "You did good, babe. She's gorgeous. She looks just like you." He swiped his soaked face with the back of his hand. "I regret so much."

Justine said, "You two have a lot to catch up on. I'm going for a walk." She grabbed her purse and scooted out the door, shutting it behind her.

Hank sat on the edge of the bed, still cradling Emily. Miranda sat next to him. He looked at his wife. "I screwed up. I am so sorry. I should have told you about the mess I made." Tears poured from his eyes. In a shaky voice he said, "Can you ever forgive me?"

"It was hard. I won't deny that. And was I mad at you. A lot." She placed her hand on his arm. "But I forgave you a while back. I wanted nothing more than to have you home with us. No one is perfect. We all make mistakes. I want us to be a family."

He looked at her through his pooled eyes. "I don't deserve you."

"Let's put Emily in her bed and then we can have time for ourselves, and you can show me how much." Miranda smiled a slight smile and gently put her hands around Emily and lifted her, taking her to the play pen bed in the corner, letting her sleep.

Hank took Miranda in his arms and kissed her like he'd lost her forever and now just found her again for the first time. They had a lot of loving to make up for.

CHAPTER FORTY-EIGHT

Meanwhile, Justine walked to a café in the middle of town. She took a table by the window. From her purse she grabbed a romance novel she'd been reading. Within moments a waitress came over and Justine ordered a piece of apple pie and coffee. She'd settle in and give Miranda and Hank some time. She could use some time to herself anyway.

She read a couple pages and then out of the corner of her eye noticed someone approaching.

"Mind if I join you?"

She looked up to find Walt, Hank's old boss, the cowboy from Cheyenne, standing in front of her. His quiet presence and his physique that seemed to speak of a lifetime of hard work, flustered her. "Uh, sure." She gestured toward the empty chair at the table.

He sat and observed her; his blue eyes marked with crow's feet that reflected the passage of time.

She put the book away in her purse. "I ordered pie and coffee if you'd like to join?"

He flagged the waitress. "I'll have what she's having." The waitress nodded and scooted toward the kitchen. She came over with two mugs and poured hot coffee in both. She reached into her apron pocket for some creamers and sugar packets. She left and returned with warm pie piled with vanilla ice cream. She set the two plates on the table.

They took their first bite. Justine said, "Mmm. This is good pie."

"Best pie in town."

"My favorite is apple. This is one of the best I've tasted. You come into town often?"

"Few times a month. I always make a stop here for Lorraine's pie. She took over when her mom retired years ago. Been one of the landmarks of Cheyenne for over forty years. But today I came to see Hank's hearing. Glad that he was released. I tried to catch up to him, but he and Miranda hurried out of the courtroom."

"What a relief. It's been a hard time for them."

"Misfortunate that it had to play out that way when they locked him up."

Justine looked at Walt as he talked, warmth and fondness in his voice.

"Want you to know, Hank's a good guy. He's no criminal. He was just trying to help out that waitress a couple years ago in that bar. Got in between her and that jerk boyfriend of hers." Walt shook his head. "Hank didn't deserve what he got. Wrong place, wrong time."

"I'll admit I was surprised at first and questioned what had happened and were we not seeing the real Hank? Had to talk to Miranda about not giving up too."

"What you see is not always what you get. Sometimes there's a back story." Walt took a bite of apple and melted ice cream.

Justine sipped her coffee. "They'll be ok. They can finally start their family and get to a sense of normal." She took another sip and set her cup down in the saucer. "You have children?"

"No. Almost married once. But most don't want to put up with a man working all hours, the hard work that comes with a ranch."

"Know what that's like. Farms and ranches are different but not that much. They both require hard work and sacrifice."

"I imagine crops have their own demands. When something needs to be done there's no putting it off."

"No. When it comes time for harvest, it's time. Stanley worked hard. We both worked hard. But I wouldn't trade it for anything."

"Same here. Nothing like working outside."

"Always thought it'd be something to go on a cattle drive."

They both finished their pie, and the waitress poured more coffee, taking their plates away. They continued chatting for an hour before Walt left for home. Justine walked back to the hotel, and on her way a lightness drifted throughout her body as she thought about how Walt had been a gentleman, respectful and kind. He had rugged charm yet seemed to have a hidden softness and vulnerability. She wondered if one day she'd be lucky enough to discover that hidden layer beneath his tough exterior.

CHAPTER FORTY-NINE

Halfway across the world, in Seoul, South Korea, Tanya competed in the 1988 Olympics. She had placed fourth in the uneven bars and hadn't placed in the vault. But her next event, the floor exercise and the balance beam were her strongest events. She had high hopes for a gold in each. Even the press was hyping her at the possibility of winning a medal in each, competing with the best in the world. They compared her skills as equal to Andreea Rosu from Romania and Katerina Petrov from the Soviet Union. Reports tagged Susan Miller and Tanya as the two from Team USA hoping to beat Andreea and Katerina.

Tanya warmed up with her team, stretching in forward bends, splits, and taking turns on the mat running through roundoff back handsprings, aerials, back summersaults and her choreography. As Tanya waited for her turn on the mat, she forced herself to mentally picture herself executing skills perfectly and sticking landings. She glanced to see Susan smiling and giving a short wave to her parents in the stands. Tanya felt a wave of sadness knowing that no one would be there to see her compete. She hadn't expected her parents to come. They had never been interested in her gymnastics, and she hardly saw them. Their marriage was too toxic to be around. She'd tried over the years to assist them. Her mom especially. But whatever she did, it never made much of a dent in helping her mom get out of the abusive environment.

Tanya was sad about not having her surrogate family, Justine and Miranda, there to see her. South Korea was thirteen hours ahead of Iowa, so it'd be 2:00 in the morning for the Graafs when she was competing in the afternoon. She couldn't expect them to stay up that late and watch her. Plus, she understood that Hank's problems came first, and she was glad Miranda could be there for him. She knew that her best friend's family was the most important. So, Tanya would do her best and bring home a medal, not only for herself but for her country, which she was so proud to represent the USA. But also, she'd bring home a medal for her family, the Graafs. She'd make them proud. She could tell them all about it when she returned to Iowa. Maybe she could show them a video or replay of the competition.

Susan flung her arms in the air at the end of her performance. It was Tanya's turn. She envisioned the passage in her routine that gave her the most difficulty. It was the landing at the end of the final movement that made her nervous. On her first run, she landed but wavered. On the second try, she landed solid. Tanya let that stick in her mind. That was how she'd do it in her competition. She could do this. She would do this.

In one corner of the gymnasium, athletes were running full speed down a runway, as they built momentum and jumped off a springboard performing twists, turns, handsprings and other skills. At another corner, athletes were swinging around and around on the uneven bars. While all this was going on, Tanya stepped up to the mat. She had to focus intently while she performed her floor exercise routine and block out any distractions.

She took a deep breath. Her heart beat double time as she stepped onto the mat. She began with a triple twist landing on the mat with a soft thud. She moved with grace and strength, tumbling from corner to corner. Before each pass, she reminded herself to point her toes, tighten her core and imagine she was the only one in the gym, like it was practice and she'd done it hundreds of times before. She mixed in sharp turns and flowing dance movements, her arms sweeping wide, drawing the attention of spectators. When she finished in a powerful double back tuck landing with a solid "stick" the crowd roared. Tanya's chest rose and fell with exhilaration, her nerves giving way to pride as she caught her breath and smiled.

She had been so worried about landing solid. She beamed. She did it. It was over. She'd done the best she could. Gave it her all.

When it came time for Tanya to compete on the balance beam, she faltered slightly on the mat after her roundoff double back flip landing. But otherwise, it was perfect. The adrenaline rush that pumped her up throughout her competition came down a few notches. Her Olympics were over. It was hard waiting to see if she won a medal. All the team stared at the scoreboard. Finally, the scores popped up. She scored a 9.950 in the floor exercise!

Tanya won a silver in the floor exercise and came in fourth on the balance beam. She did it! She won a medal.

Tanya had given everything she had. As she stood on the podium to receive her medal her eyes filled, knowing this was the end of her gymnastics career. All the years and hours of practice coming to an end. She may not be giving up on gymnastics completely. But the Olympics were the ultimate. Her ultimate goal. And she was twenty-six, too old for a gymnast. She didn't know what she would do next. But tears streamed down her cheeks at the pride she felt in representing her country. She would have liked to get gold so she could have heard the Star-Spangled Banner from USA, but she'd take the silver with pride.

CHAPTER FIFTY

In the middle of the night, Miranda, Hank, and Justine huddled in Justine's living room watching the Olympics intently on TV. Miranda squeezed Hank's hand as they focused on Tanya's every move through each event. They cheered loudly, hugging and crying when Tanya won her silver medal.

Justine wiped tears of pride and joy from her eyes. "Our girl won a medal. I knew she could do it. I'm so proud of Tanya."

Miranda nodded, tears falling on top of Emily as she nursed. "I hope her parents are watching."

"All that she'd been through, with her broken ankle and her parents' difficulties. She's a trooper."

"She's strong inside and out."

Hank smiled and looked at his family. He felt so blessed he could share this moment now and every moment in the future with them.

When Miranda finished nursing Emily, Hank lifted the baby up and onto his chest, patted her back gently, burping her. What a huge miracle he could do this. He'd only been out of jail two days, and it still felt surreal to be free. Freedom was a big deal. You didn't know how big until you'd had your freedom taken away. The fact that his attorney found the truth about his ordeal with the planted drugs made all the difference. Otherwise, he may have had to be in jail years more, not just months for something he had nothing to do with. Life could be unfair. But it could also have many blessings. You just had to look for them.

When they finished watching Tanya in the Olympics, Miranda and Hank went to their house and slept in. In the morning, they dropped off Emily at Justine's for a few hours and headed for the barn. Hank was anxious to see the horses and make plans for his business of raising and training Quarter Horses. They held hands as they trekked to the barn and chatted about their future. It felt amazing to be together again. Hank couldn't get enough of Miranda, and he was amazed at how much he loved his daughter. He was excited to begin their bright future. Miranda looked at him, squeezed his hand and smiled. He was a lucky man.

As they approached the barn, a dually traveled toward them. A tall blond man got out of the truck and held a big dog in his arms.

Miranda waved and greeted the man walking toward her. "Hi Gerrit. What can I help you with?"

Hank saw the way this tall herculean guy looked at his wife. They seemed too familiar with each other as they talked about the patient between them.

Miranda gestured. "Honey, this is Gerrit, a large animal vet from Clinton. We've been helping each other out the past few months."

Hercules nodded and shifted the large dog in his arms. "You must be Hank. I've heard lots about you. I bet you're glad to be back."

Hank felt his face growing hot. Both with embarrassment and irritation that his wife had been sharing about their life and problems. He reached out to shake Gerrit's hand. Hercules shifted the large dog in his arms and met Hank's grip.

Miranda glanced back and forth between the men. "Gerrit, bring him inside and we'll take a look." She headed for her clinic door. Hercules followed her inside.

Hank walked behind them. He wasn't the jealous type but something about this guy bugged him. He didn't trust him. The looks Hercules gave Miranda and the way he'd been taking up space, Hank's space, when he had been in jail, boiled Hank's blood.

They all stood around the stainless table as Miranda examined the big collie. Hank felt especially out of place. It wasn't helping the feelings inside him rolling around in his belly like a lottery cage spinning the numbers before plucking out a winner. Being here next to this big guy, half a foot over six feet, was making Hank want to grab his shirt and ask him what his intentions were. Hank had learned a lot of crude and animal-like behaviors. Things were solved with fists, not words. He'd been in jail for five months but not that long that he'd lost his sense of decency. He cleared his throat. "I'm going to leave you to it. I want to see how the horses are doing."

Miranda looked up; her face blushed. "Ok, see you out there in a few."

Hank saw the discomfort and awkward feelings on Miranda's face. Did anything happen between her and Hercules? He trusted Miranda but he also knew it was hard for her when he was gone. He'd messed up. He couldn't blame her if she had started something with him. He hated the idea of it and prayed that nothing had happened.

In the barn, he went to Red's stall. "Hey, big guy." As he ran his hand along Red's withers, the big horse nickered and rubbed his face on Hank's arm.

Hank grabbed the halter and lead rope off the wall beside the door and slipped the halter over Red's head. He hooked the rope to the ring under his chin. He led him out to the grooming area and hooked a rope on either side of the horse's head. As Hank brushed and groomed his horse, he thought about all that he'd missed while he was gone. He knew he had a lot of making up to do with Miranda and Emily too. He'd missed her birth. Her first moments in the world. He'd missed those sleepless nights sharing them with Miranda. She'd had to do that all by herself. Emily slept most of the night now. Those first bites of real food. Sitting up and crawling. Holding and rocking his first born. Her first babbles. Her first smiles.

Hank rubbed the back of his hand over his eyes. He couldn't get soft now. That was the last thing that he needed to do. It wouldn't bring that time back. So, he might as well dry up and get on with it. He would do everything he needed to do to make up for missed time.

CHAPTER FIFTY-ONE

Miranda worked side by side with Gerrit as they stitched up the cuts on the collie's leg. The dog had gotten into a fight with a racoon. Gerrit had given the collie a shot earlier to sedate him. They worked quickly before the drug wore off.

Miranda reviewed the encounter with Gerrit, Hank, and herself at the edge of the barn when Gerrit arrived. She had felt so uncomfortable. Her whole body heated up mostly from the awkwardness of Hank meeting Gerrit. It had been a weird few months working with Gerrit while Hank was gone. She probably shared too much about Hank with Gerrit. He was a good listener.

But luckily, she caught herself before things went too far at the conference and she realized just how much Hank meant to her. It could have turned out much worse. She hoped Hank didn't think there was something going on between her and Gerrit. The thought of hurting Hank sickened her. The look Hank gave her before he went out into the barn was one of quiet resignation. There were questions behind his eyes, and the answers would have to wait before they could talk and figure things out. It had been a couple days of reconnecting and getting to know each other again after time apart. They had been apart before when she was in Europe, yet this time Hank's distance was loaded with guilt and blame and regrets.

He had apologized over and over again to her in the last two days. She forgave him. Or had she completely?

The one thing she was certain of was that she wanted to spend the rest of their lives together as a family, moving past the rocky start of their marriage. Hopefully, years from now when they were old and gray they would snicker about the tough times and look back with admiration and love knowing they had stuck together through better and worse.

Miranda heard a commotion outside and just as she was sewing the last stitch in the Collie's paw she looked at Gerrit. "I need to go see what's going on. You got this?"

He nodded. "Go. I'll get this big guy ready to take back to my office. I got it from here."

Miranda scooted outside to find one of the horses loose, trotting around the barnyard. Stephanie, Larry, and Hank were trying to catch him. They each stood in a corner of the yard, blocking the way for the horse to move beyond them and on down the driveway and onto the main road. It could cause an accident if the horse got in the way of a car.

Miranda noticed it was one of the boarders. A Palomino.

Stephanie ran over to her. "I'm sorry, Miranda. I was getting Blondie out of the pasture, and she slipped away before I could put her halter on."

"It happens. Maybe she got spooked."

Stephanie followed Miranda toward the center of the backyard. Just when Blondie headed down the driveway toward the road, Hank yelled out and gave a command in a firm voice, "Ho." Luckily, she halted in her tracks. Hank rushed to the horse's side and flipped a rope around her neck.

Miranda said, "Thank goodness her owner trained her to halt. Not every horse knows that command."

Stephanie hurried to give Hank the halter she had taken out to the pasture to get Blondie in the first place. Hank put it on the mare's butterscotch head and led her toward the barn.

CHAPTER FIFTY-TWO

That afternoon, Stephanie assisted Miranda as she vaccinated the horses. In the summer and early fall months horses typically receive core vaccinations: tetanus, Eastern and Western encephalomyelitis, rabies, influenza, herpesvirus, and Potomac Horse Fever, depending on each horse's situation. Hank observed at a distance as he picked at the frog on the bottom of Red's foot. Usually, Hank would help Miranda when she gave the horses shots, but he realized as he watched, she had everything covered and different people had covered for him. Larry was filling the feed buckets in each of the stalls. Hank felt like he had been replaceable in only a few months.

His thoughts trotted back to Gerrit. Was he replacing Hank? Had Miranda allowed Gerrit to take Hank's role before he was released from jail? Transitioning back to life as a free man was harder than he thought. They needed to talk and figure things out. But it seemed that things got in the way. Since he'd returned home a few days prior it had gone from watching Tanya in the Olympics to taking care of Emily whom he adored. And now the veterinarian practice took forefront. Getting used to these demands would take time.

When he was in jail, Hank spent time on work release staying out of the way of guys that were a magnet for trouble. But he had never raised a child before and babies took a lot of attention. He'd been up a couple times during the night when Emily was crying, waking Miranda and him up. He tried to help Miranda as much as he could. But Miranda had done this all on her own for five months. She had it down.

He offered to hold Emily when she finished feeding her, but Miranda had said, "Thanks, but we've got this. Why don't you go back to bed?"

Everywhere he turned, Hank felt dejected and like he had been replaced and wasn't needed. He'd have to figure a way to blend back into civilian life and into his family. He felt overwhelmed. He wanted to spend time with Miranda and mend their relationship. The time apart had brought an awkwardness to their marriage. He wanted to get to know Emily and to learn how to be a good dad. His own father hadn't given him a model, and he'd have to figure it out. He'd have to be patient. He knew that. But he wanted desperately to go back to the way things were before he went to jail. But things were different now. He had a family, and he need to start acting like a man that had a family. Miranda wouldn't want someone who was feeling sorry for himself. He needed to step it up. Hank gently let go of Red's hind hoof and the big horse slowly settled his leg onto the cement surface of the barn.

CHAPTER FIFTY-THREE

Later that day after a long day of vaccinating horses, treating a dog that had been hit by a car, and tending to the patients in her clinic, Miranda finally sat at her desk. Emily was at her mom's. She took a couple minutes before she went to get her, closed her eyes and took a breath. It had been a whirlwind day. Hank was home. She felt relieved, and yet something nagged at her. Hank seemed so unsettled and uncomfortable being home. She knew it was going to be a big adjustment. She knew he was glad to be home. He'd told her many times about how lucky he was and how much he loved her and Emily. But there was something weighing on him and it felt awkward being together. It had been five months apart, but had it changed him so much they couldn't find their way back to each other? Her heart felt heavy thinking about spring and summer. She should feel overjoyed that Hank was home. She was happy but it had changed him. He seemed so closed off and shut down. Maybe being locked up had done a number on him.

She needed to be understanding and patient. It would take time for him to integrate back into their world. And it would take time for them to find each other again. She hated what happened to him, to them. She hated it and she was still angry about all of it. But Hank was human, and he could make mistakes like anyone else. They definitely needed to have a talk, but it seemed like things got in the way since he'd returned home a few days ago. They'd have to make time. Just then, Hank stepped into her office from the side barn door. They looked at each other, both silent for a few moments. Hank opened his mouth to speak and the phone on Miranda's desk rang.

She glanced at the phone. "I'll let the answering machine get it."

"Answer it. We can talk later."

"Dr. Graaf." She laughed. "Tanya! I'm so proud of you."

Hank turned and headed back into the barn, closing the door behind him. *Later. They'd talk later.* He went to his horse, saddled him up and led him outside. He'd go for a ride to clear his head. When he got back, they could have a talk. Once he mounted the big red horse, he felt the breeze hit his face and breathed in fresh air. The air in jail had been stale, putrid at times, unwashed men and foul air from the dark and negative energy surrounding him for months. He felt cleaner somehow as he rode, the outside air and the rhythm of the clomp, clomp of his horse, releasing all the negativity from his body and soul. It had been what he'd needed all along. He'd forgotten how he loved riding and how free it made him feel.

As he rode into the woods he remembered when he was out for a long ride before he and Miranda got together. She was on a ride with Tanya and the picture of her on Mandy flooded his thoughts. He chuckled thinking about how Mandy nickered when Hank gave her some sugar. Miranda had been so righteous about not feeding her horse sugar, that it was bad for her. And how indignant she was when Mandy showed him affection and nuzzled his hand. He remembered the sensations in his body, his love for Miranda began simmering then and he had tried so hard to tamp it down. She was with someone else then. He didn't have business pursuing her. And yet look where he was now. Married to the love of his life. The universe had conspired to get them together after all.

They'd been through some hard stuff already in their young marriage. And they were still together.

He smiled and kept riding. Red took him to the pond, Miranda and Hank's favorite place. His big red head bowed down and he sipped water from the pond. They stood there for several minutes, Hank looking at the evening sun starting to mute its brightness. He turned in his saddle to the flicker of the brush behind. A jolt of surprise ran through him as he spotted Miranda in the opening of the trail, sun shining on her golden hair, falling to one side. She was so beautiful.

Miranda urged Mandy toward Hank's side at the edge of the pond. "Howdy, stranger."

"Hi, beautiful."

"I think we have some catching up to do."

"Now is as good a time as any."

They sat on their horses for a few minutes looking out at the pond, the setting sun reflecting on the water, their favorite place they'd go to, strengthening their bond each time they returned home. But it seemed like a lifetime with their marriage hanging in the wings before one of them spoke.

Hank spoke first: "I am so sorry, Miranda, from the bottom of my heart that I did what I did. Mostly that I didn't tell you about what happened before it was too late, and they were hauling me off to jail."

Miranda opened her mouth to speak. Hank held up his hand. "Please let me finish everything I have to say."

She nodded.

"It was selfish of me to leave you out. We're married and we're meant to share everything and be a part of everything. I was afraid that you'd be angry with me and really, I was afraid you'd reject me if you knew that I had once been in jail and that the law was coming after me." He drew in a deep breath. "But in the end, I made a huge mess of things. And I feel regret, shame, and anger at myself for letting it go that far."

She put her hand on his arm. "Thank you for apologizing. It's been hard, you not being here with us. It was like I was a single parent, like you deserted your family. I thought about how you told me you didn't want to be like your father, leaving your family. And here you were doing the same thing. At times I didn't know how to cope and would just plow ahead. I also got help from a lot of people: Larry and Stephanie, Tanya and Nash, of course my mom."

"And Gerrit."

"Yes. Gerrit."

Hank's heart pounded, nearly leaping out of his chest. "I got to admit, when he pulled in the driveway I didn't like it. I wasn't jealous but I felt left out when you two were treating that dog." Neither one said anything for a few beats. "Should I be worried, Miranda?"

"He has helped me out a lot and I like Gerrit. I've learned a lot from him, how he conducts his practice. How he takes care of horses. And for a brief minute I started to have feelings for him. But when I was at a conference in Ames, I realized how much I wanted things to work with us."

Hank searched her face.

She looked at him, and with a slight smile, said, "I realized how much you mean to me." She leaned in her saddle and cupped his face with her hand. "How much I love you."

A frown formed between his eyebrows. "Did anything happen between you two? I would understand if it did."

"No. Nothing happened."

Hank released the huge ball of air that had been trapped in his chest. "I want to spend the rest of my life making it up to you, babe."

She moved her head once to the left and then to the right. "I don't want you to live like that, like you're indebted to me. I want to make a fresh start for our family."

He leaned closer to Miranda and bent to kiss her. He held her hand. "You are the most amazing woman. I don't deserve you. I love you so much."

Her lips meshed with his. "I want to leave the past behind us and move forward. I love you." The sun setting formed a silhouette of them holding hands and kissing in the shadows as they sat on their horses, beginning the first day of their new life together.

Hank finally said, "Let's go and get our beautiful daughter at your mom's."

They turned their horses and headed home.

CHAPTER FIFTY-FOUR

The first week in October Tanya finally was able to fly home after the closing ceremonies at the Olympics. On the plane from South Korea to Chicago she had several hours to think about the last few weeks at the games. It was the most amazing experience she had ever had. All the people she met and the friends she made she was certain she'd keep in contact with. The gymnasts from other countries were her competition but they were very similar people. They were athletic of course but also had the same ambitions and goals. The language barrier made it difficult to communicate at times, but she got to know a few of them after the gymnastics portion of the games were over.

Tanya thought about how she'd wished she had had someone who knew her from home. She felt sad, Miranda and Justine weren't there. Sadder than not having her parents present to congratulate her and see her win the silver medal. Her brothers weren't there but she wasn't surprised about that. She and her family were strangers, and except for her mom, they hadn't spoken in a couple of years. It was nice talking to Miranda on the phone and knowing that they saw her compete. At least there was that.

But it felt anticlimactic going home. What would she do now? She had no idea. Maybe she could help Miranda while

Tanya figured it out. They could always use help on the farm. Her thoughts drifted to the breakup she'd had with Daniel. Surprisingly, she didn't miss him at all and never thought about watching him compete. She didn't see him the whole time she was in South Korea, except for the closing ceremonies when USA walked together gathered in teams. She glanced a peek at him and heard that he hadn't even won a medal. Hmm. Served him right for being so mean to her.

Tanya closed her eyes, willing herself to sleep and instead, thought about Nash. His hungry eyes, clear and gray, an open door to his soul. She longed to touch his scruffy black beard, breathing in his musky scent. She had thought about him a lot while she was in South Korea. She hoped he could have been there but that would be ridiculous. They weren't even dating. Sure, they had had several moments. But nothing came of it. She had to admit to herself. She wished it had. She couldn't get him out of her mind. Her pulse surged as she thought of kissing him and what it would be like, holding him close and it sent shivers that frolicked all over her body. He captivated her and made her feel things that did her in. In a good way.

By the time they landed in Chicago she was exhausted and exhilarated. She hadn't slept much on the long flight. But she was excited to be home in the USA. She missed it while she was away. Just being in the US felt like home, before she even got to Iowa.

When she boarded the plane taking her from Chicago for the hour flight to the Quad Cities it dawned on her she hadn't made arrangements for someone to pick her up. And where was home exactly? She thought she'd go to Miranda's first. But was there room for her now that Hank was home? *Agh*, she hadn't planned ahead.

She decided she'd call Miranda when they landed. And then she'd go from there. She could count on her bestie to pick her up. She leaned back in her seat.

The flight attendant pushing the cart for drinks stopped at Tanya's seat. She looked at her and said, "You're that gymnast that won a silver aren't you? Tanya Miller?"

Tanya felt herself blushing and nodded.

The flight attendant took a napkin off the cart and a pen from her pocket. "Could I get an autograph?"

Tanya signed the napkin, then gave it back. There was so much activity the last few days in Seoul that she hadn't had time to let it sink in that people might recognize her. Tanya was thrilled to win a silver medal but didn't think it earned her a place in the world to be famous. She'd signed a few autographs before she headed home in South Korea, but she didn't think anyone would notice when she returned to America.

After an hour, the plane began its decent onto the Quad Cities airport runway in Molline, Illinois. She could see the Mississippi from her window and the golden corn fields on either side of the river stretching the multitude of acres of farmland both in Illinois and Iowa. Tanya took note of the parking lot, full of cars. For a small airport she was surprised to see it so busy.

The airplane landed and taxied to the gate. Once the plane came to a complete stop, the flight attendant made an announcement that they were ready to deboard. Tanya gathered her purse and backpack and walked down the aisle with the other passengers. They exited the airplane and continued along the ramp leading to the inside of the airport.

Tanya stepped off the ramp into a large room and was blasted by a large crowd cheering and clapping and holding a banner reading *Welcome home, Olympian, our Tanya.*

Tanya's breath caught in her throat. She clapped a hand to her mouth. Tears spouted from her eyes. She couldn't believe it. All these people were waiting for *her*. She had thought no one cared and she felt sorry for herself the whole way home.

Miranda stepped through the crowd rushing to Tanya. She hugged her tightly. "Welcome home, Tonny. We love ya, girl. You're our town hero."

"I can't believe it. All these people." Tanya walked toward the crowd.

Pastor Bob was there with a big smile on his face. "Congratulations, Tanya. You made our town proud." He shook her hand.

Hank stood beside him, holding Emily. "You were great. Congratulations."

Tanya said, "Thanks, Hank. I'm glad you're finally home." She lightly shook Emily's foot. "Emily, you've gotten so big."

Miranda followed Tanya as she went to greet people. Hank and Emily came after Miranda and then moved toward the back of the crowd. Larry and Stephanie, both gave her a hug. Larry said, "You're all Stephanie can talk about these days. She wants to join the college gymnastics team."

Stephanie beamed. Her face reddened as she shyly looked at Tanya, in awe being in the presence of this small-town celebrity.

Tanya continued moving through the crowd. Mrs. Van Buren swooped in for a bear hug, Tanya's face getting lost in the tall woman's chest. Mrs. Van Buren said, "We are so proud of you. You were amazing in South Korea. Watching you flip through the air on the beam and that floor routine. Whew, made me dizzy. I don't know how you do it." She released the hug and looked at Tanya. "You've got this town buzzing."

Miranda led Tanya to Rex, Miranda's uncle and his boyfriend Rodney. They held out hands to shake. "Congratulations, Tanya."

"Thank you so much for coming. All the way from California? I'm beside myself."

"We wouldn't miss it. You make our whole country proud."

Next to them stood the Bishops and the Browns, next door neighbors of Miranda. Mrs. Brown, standing next to Hank, leaned in and said, "Your secrets safe with me, Hank."

He gave her a quizzical look.

She raised her index finger. "I was there that day you got hauled away by the police."

Hank just nodded, knowing that his stint in jail would follow him for the rest of his life one way or another. In his mind he shook the dark thoughts away and carried on with the celebration of the hour.

There were a lot of other neighbors and friends to greet. After several minutes of talking to people and hearing *"Job well done!"* and *"Congratulations!"* Tanya stepped in front of the crowd and said, "Thank you everyone. I am blown away." Tears streamed down her face. "I had no idea…"

As her eyes scanned the crowd, way in the back, her heart thumped over a fence and stopped. Nash was standing in the corner at the rear of the room. Her heartbeat raced like a horse galloping through a field. The crowd parted as she walked to the back towards him. When she reached Nash, and he looked at her with those clear gray eyes she wanted to leap into his arms and have him carry her away.

In a deep voice that soothed her soul he said, "Hey, Tanya. Welcome home."

She gently clasped her hands around his face, and he bent, pulling her close and kissed her, his scruffy beard tickling her chin. She leaned into him as they blended into a moment of a dream that she'd been waiting for a long time to come true. Yes. In his arms she was finally home.

Justine stood near Walt as they watched all that took place in this gathering of friends, family and neighbors. Justine said, "Out of hardship, dreams really can come true."

Walt nodded. "Lots of love in this room."

Miranda and Hank walked hand in hand to Tanya and Nash. Hank said, "Come on lovebirds, let's all go back to the farm."

Miranda said, "We've got lots to celebrate."

ACKNOWLEDGMENTS

Writing the last book of the Dreams Trilogy has been quite a ride, and I truly appreciate all the readers who have patiently waited for the conclusion about the Graaf family's story, especially, Hank. Writing about the Graaf's has become a big part of me and I'm sad to put my pen down for this amazing family and their life adventures. So, thank you so much for taking the time to read Unshakable Dreams!

Please let me know what you think about this book by emailing me or posting a review on Amazon. It helps me so much knowing what you think as I write more books about heart and home!

Thank you to Geoff Affleck once again for his expertise while publishing my third book.

Thank you, a million times over to Alissia J. R. Lingaur for your wisdom and talent as an editor joining me in my writing journey. I have learned so much from you.

To Peter, my love and partner in life, thank you for your endless support and pep talks throughout my writing career.

Elizabeth Ann Thompson lives in northern Michigan with her husband surrounded by farms, lakes, forests, and small towns. Elizabeth enjoys writing about romance and family in simpler times before she learned how to use a computer or cell phone. When she's not writing she enjoys going on long walks and finding the best bakeries to fulfill her passion for cookies and pie.

Follow Elizabeth Ann Thompson on social media and be the first to know when her next release is available:

Websites: elizabethannthompson.net &

pursueyourdreams.net

Instagram: elizabethannthompson20

Facebook: Elizabeth Ann Thompson – Author

www.ingramcontent.com/pod-product-compliance
Lightning Source LLC
Chambersburg PA
CBHW032259310726
48973CB00008B/2453